"Stefanie," Jesse pleaded, "look at me."

She obeyed, her eyes wide and vulnerable, her face framed by wind-tangled hair. He stroked her cheek. "I hurt you last night, and I'm sorry. I shouldn't have assumed that because you were older you were...willing."

Stefanie winced and pulled away from him. She *had* been willing, instinctively passionate. What should have been a beautiful, shared experience had been shattered because of her past. "It wasn't just y-you," she whispered unsteadily, staring along the beach. "S-something happened a long t-time ago. I should have told you...." Helplessly she stopped.

How could she begin to recount the emotional devastation that had been the basis of her reaction last night?

WELCOME
TO THE WONDERFUL WORLD
OF *Harlequin Romances*

Interesting, informative and entertaining,
each Harlequin Romance portrays an appealing
and original love story. With a varied array
of settings, we may lure you on an African safari,
to a quaint Welsh village, or an exotic Riviera
location—anywhere and everywhere that adventurous
men and women fall in love.

As publishers of Harlequin Romances, we're
extremely proud of our books. Since 1949,
Harlequin Enterprises has built its publishing
reputation on the solid base of quality and
originality. Our stories are the most popular
paperback romances sold in North America; every
month, six new titles are released and sold at
nearly every book-selling store in Canada and the
United States.

For a list of all titles currently available,
send your name and address to:

HARLEQUIN READER SERVICE,
(In the U.S.) P.O. Box 52040, Phoenix, AZ 85072-2040
(In Canada) P.O. Box 2800, Postal Station A
5170 Yonge Street, Willowdale, Ont.   M2N 6J3

We sincerely hope you enjoy reading
this Harlequin Romance.

Yours truly,

THE PUBLISHERS
Harlequin Romances

The Turn of the Tide

Samantha Day

Harlequin Books

TORONTO • NEW YORK • LONDON
AMSTERDAM • PARIS • SYDNEY • HAMBURG
STOCKHOLM • ATHENS • TOKYO • MILAN

Original hardcover edition published in 1984
by Mills & Boon Limited

ISBN 0-373-02672-2

Harlequin Romance first edition February 1985

CHAPTER ONE

'APPARENTLY she's a real power freak—y'know, gets turned on by money and position.'

Stefanie Hart grimaced with disgust at the words drifting in through the partially open office door. *Madge again,* she thought as she continued her impatient search through the file drawer. *I wonder who's getting the knife today?* She listened absently, more concerned with finding the file she needed to complete the report waiting on her desk.

'How do you think she got where she is anyhow?' The words were sharp with excitement. 'There were others more qualified for the job, y'know. Although,' Madge snickered crudely, 'Old Man Cummins seems to think she's qualified enough in certain areas, if y'know what I mean!'

Stefanie's fingers stilled their search and her lips tightened. She knew only too well what Madge meant— and who she was talking about. She straightened up slowly and walked quietly to the door.

'Still, it's Tony Barrow I feel sorry for.' There was a loud sigh of sympathy. 'They used to go together, y'know—till he found out what was going on behind his back!'

Stefanie had heard enough. She pushed the door open and leaned against the frame, watching the two women huddled around the desk in the outer office. Madge's companion saw her first. She stared at Stefanie for a shocked moment, saw the strong expression of contempt on her face, and fled.

Madge turned around slowly, knowing who must be standing behind her. Her face was a mottled red and her mouth gaped open, soundless for once. Stefanie watched her squirm, fighting down the words of anger that boiled inside her. Hateful as she was, Madge merely carried the gossip—the whispers started elsewhere. Stefanie straightened up slowly and said coldly, 'I want the file I requested before lunch on my desk—immediately.' She made no attempt to hide her disgust. She waited until Madge had scuttled past her into the file room and then walked away, stiff with anger, to the privacy of her own office.

Damn Tony! Stefanie clenched her hands at her sides and stared out of the office window at the white winter scene, tears of rage pricking the corners of her eyes. He's not going to give up, she realised with despair, knowing that the insinuations, the out-and-out lies she had unwittingly overheard could only have originated with him. He was slowly and insidiously destroying her reputation and credibility within the firm. Scowling with angry frustration, Stefanie turned away from the window and paced the narrow width of the room.

All the gossip and speculation about her promotion should have died a normal office death by now, but it hadn't. After almost three months, the ugly rumours were kept alive and circulating. 'I know you're doing it, Tony,' Stefanie muttered under her breath. 'You and that bitchy little Dawna!' She stopped her pacing in mid-stride and glanced at her watch. One-thirty! She groaned with despair. There was no way she was going to calm down enough to make it through the rest of the day.

She hesitated for a moment, looking down at the auditor's report waiting on her desk. To hell with it, she thought, suddenly mutinous, and sat down to pull a pair of black leather boots over her slim legs. To hell with the whole place! Her anger and disgust squashed any guilt she might have felt for leaving early. She slid her arms into a white Icelandic wool coat, jammed a green mohair hat on her head, and walked from her office.

The receptionist looked up in surprise. 'Leaving already?'

'I'm sick,' Stefanie said shortly, without even glancing at the girl. Sick and tried of you lot and your petty little games, she added silently, and pushed open the outer door with unusual force.

She ignored the bus she usually took to save on downtown parking fees and started to walk home. As the heat of her anger cooled, the cold February air began to penetrate, chasing away all thoughts but those of the comfort and warmth of her waiting apartment. With a shiver, she quickened her pace, her boots squeaking and crunching over the snow-packed sidewalk. As she crossed the bridge under a blast of Arctic wind she scolded herself soundly for dressing for the office and not a Winnipeg winter. Almost running, she took a short cut through a parking lot and headed for her apartment building.

She fumbled with numb fingers for a moment before she was able to turn her key in the frozen lock. Finally the door opened and with a sigh of relief, she slipped into her apartment and slammed the door on the frigid air. She kicked off her boots, hung up her coat and headed for the kitchen. In no time she was warming her fingers around a hot cup of coffee.

'Move, cat,' she said, pushing the huge black animal from his favourite position on her favourite chair. With a sleepy yawn, the cat stretched and eyed her balefully before curling up on the rug and promptly falling back to sleep.

'Lazy animal,' Stefanie murmured absently as she took his place in the big armchair. She stretched her legs out in front of her, feeling only a residue of the anger that had stormed through her at the office. Funny how thawing out always makes me feel so sleepy, she thought as she sipped her coffee. Stifling a yawn, she put her mug down and laid her head against the back of the chair. She closed her eyes and relaxed, beginning to enjoy the unexpected time off.

She was beginning to feel as though all she ever did was work, as though her whole life was revolving around the office. Until last week she had attended accounting classes two evenings a week, worked late at least one other night, and studied in between. And for what? she thought angrily. For the rest of the staff to whisper about how I got the job because I sleep with the boss!

With this bitter thought, Stefanie got up. It all came back to Tony and his lies. She crossed the living room and knelt on the thick carpet under the window, staring out on the winter stillness. The banks of the Assiniboine River sloped from just outside her apartment, covered with ice and snow. Directly across the frozen river, through a barrier of barren elm trees, she could see the Legislative Buildings. She sighed and rested her head on her arms as she watched a lone cross-country skier on the snow-covered river. Damn Tony, she thought again, with more sadness than anger.

'How could I have been so wrong about him, Pete?' she asked the cat, who, except for a twitch of an ear, slept on. Usually her judgment was reliable and fairly accurate. It had failed her miserably with Tony.

She had met him when he started working for the accounting firm that employed her. The attraction was immediate between the two junior members. Stefanie was drawn to his wit and boyish good looks, enjoying his company enormously. The only real flaw in their relationship was his periodical attempt to try and get her to sleep with him. She resisted with her usual ease and Tony, with an indifferent shrug that belied his frustration, would resume their normal, almost platonic relationship. It was enough for Stefanie to have him as a very good friend.

The friendship ended suddenly with an announcement of a promotion for Stefanie. Their boss, J. J. Cummins, chose to honour her with the news at a staff Christmas party. She had turned to Tony, excitement lighting her eyes, and had found a white-faced stranger standing beside her. He hadn't offered congratulations. In fact, he hadn't said a word. He had looked at her—through her, Stefanie remembered with a shudder—turned abruptly, and walked away.

Within the hour he had been dancing with one of the secretaries. Dawna Hobson was a cute little sex kitten who dressed for the office like most people would dress for a night club, and her outfit that night was truly outrageous. Their behaviour on the dance floor would have attracted attention even if people hadn't known that Stefanie and Tony were usually a couple. They danced close and drank fast, their loud laughter and pointed looks in Stefanie's direction obvious to all. It wasn't long before more speculative glances joined theirs.

Proud but hurting, Stefanie managed to confront Tony before the night was over. His attack was brief and vicious. The promotion should have been his, he told her, and added with a cruel sneer that if he didn't know from experience how frigid she was, he would assume she had got the job by sleeping with the boss. In fact, he had speculated with a leer, maybe she wasn't so frigid when it came to giving sex for favours granted. Stunned and hurt beyond words, Stefanie had recoiled from his assault and slipped quietly away from the party.

She had spent Christmas alone. All her plans had been made with Tony and there just wasn't anyone else. She quietly and somewhat sadly spent the day reminiscing with old photo albums and letters her father had written to her before his death two years before.

Returning to work after the holidays was hard. Whatever Tony had said worked. Her co-workers were suspicious and distant, but Stefanie's pride came to the rescue. Her pretty mouth tightened into a harder line and the whimsical look in her eyes was replaced by a glint of determination. Determination to act as though Tony's defection and the ugly rumours that followed didn't matter; determination to show the doubters that she could do the job and do it well. Long hours of competent work put rest to the worst of the rumours, that she had obtained her promotion through sexual favours given the boss. Or so she thought until today. The awful words she had overheard came rushing back. Why couldn't they just drop it?

Because Tony wouldn't let them, she realised dejectedly, and stood up slowly. She scooped up the big cat and rubbed her cheek against his soft fur. 'I can't fight it any more, Pete. I don't know what I'm going to do about it, but I'm not going to sit around all weekend moping about it. I'm going out!'

She didn't. With a sigh, she hung up the telephone yet again. What was happening to all her friends? They were scattering fast, moving, getting married ... She closed the address book and resigned herself to an evening with a book or television, but in reality she couldn't relax enough to do either. She was filled with a restless energy that couldn't be channelled.

'Midwinter blues,' she assured herself, knowing even as she said it, that it went deeper than that. It was a strange feeling, a vague anticipation combined with a growing dissatisfaction with the route her life was taking. She frowned and nibbled her thumbnail reflectively. It was time to sit down and re-assess her life.

It didn't take Stefanie long to realise what she had to do. What took time was talking herself into it. She wasn't inclined to do things impulsively, and after all, her life was really quite comfortable, wasn't it?

'No, it's not!' she answered herself emphatically. She could stay where she was, alone with her cat while making her way to the top in a job that was making her miserable, or she could quit and start over. Just another job? Stefanie stared out the window for the umpteenth time that weekend. Why not another city?

On Monday morning she handed in her resignation. She was blunt about her reasons for leaving, and without giving names, told Mr Cummins the truth. She watched with satisfaction as her boss went through the stages from embarrassment to anger as he listened to her telling of his supposed duplicity. The man was astute: He would get to the bottom of things quickly enough now that he knew what was going on, but it was too late for Stefanie. She was adamant about leaving and Mr Cummins accepted her resignation reluctantly. He promised her a good recommendation before agreeing that she could take her holidays in lieu of notice.

Stefanie returned to her own office, cleaned out her desk and left without a backward glance. Her step was light and her eyes brighter than they had been for a long time. She drove home quickly and walked into the apartment. 'It's done, Pete,' she laughed at the cat rubbing against her legs. 'I'm free—where should we go?'

She chose to go west. She had travelled extensively in Eastern Canada, but had never been farther west than one skiing trip to Banff in the heart of the Canadian Rockies. Revelling in her freedom and feeling adventurous, she decided without much hesitation to go as far west as she could. Vancouver, she thought with a gleam of anticipation in her clear eyes, here I come!

Spring comes earlier to the West Coast of British Columbia than to the rest of Canada, and after a fifteen-hundred-mile drive across snow-swept prairie and mountain, Stefanie delighted in the burgeoning verdancy of Vancouver. She was able to find a promising new job within days of her arrival, and was told, to her further joy, that she need not start until April.

Knowing that the practical thing to do in the meantime was to find an apartment and settle in, Stefanie perversely did the opposite. Blowing a fair-sized chunk of her savings, she arranged for the rental of a cottage on Vancouver Island, as close to the ocean as she could get. Quickly packing items that would add to her enjoyment in what promised to be luxurious accommodation, she drove her well packed car to the ferry at Horseshoe Bay. Two hours later she was on the Island.

It was a long drive, more because of twisting mountain roads than actual distance. Several hours after she had left the ferry at Nanaimo, she found the turn-off from the highway to her cottage. She pulled the car to a stop under the towering cedar trees that lined the driveway and got out, glad to ease her cramped muscles. The cat, waking as soon as the engine stopped, jumped out after her, stretched, and sniffed the air delicately.

'This is a cottage?' Stefanie asked out loud, standing in front of the well designed house. 'Fantastic!'

She pulled a key chain from her shoulder bag and

started up the stone walkway, then stopped suddenly. She stood thoughtfully weighing the key in one hand, looking from the house to the car. The logical thing to do, she thought, was to unpack and settle in. She sighed, reaching up to rub sore neck muscles, remembering the load she had packed in Vancouver that morning—everything from groceries and suitcases full of clothes to boxes of books and records, even her stereo packed carefully on the back seat.

'Yuck,' she said with a grimace, and turned towards the ocean. She could hear it, smell it and even feel it in the dampness of the air, and was dying to see it. It was no decision. The unpacking could wait. She scooped up the cat and tossed him back in the car. 'Sorry, Pete,' she said, 'but I've been on the West Coast for exactly one week and the closest I've been to the water is the ferry ride from Vancouver. I'm going to the beach!' She closed the door on his yowl of protest, flipped the keys into her jacket pocket and was off, following the sound of pounding surf.

There was a sandy path leading around the house through the trees. Stefanie stopped for a moment at the front and stared at the architect's delight that was to be her home for the next six weeks. It was shaped so that it seemed to rise from the forest floor like the hemlock and cedar trees that surrounded it. The entire front consisted of long slender windows in narrow frames that stretched to the peak of the weathered cedar roof. It wasn't large, but had been designed to fit perfectly into the woody landscape. The underbrush had been cleared from the front, giving the yard a parklike appearance through which was seen a tantalising view of sand and surf.

Stefanie was torn for a moment between exploring the house or the beach. Again, it was no real decision. She ran lightly through the trees, stopped with delight when she came to the beach. The whole outer edge of the sand was rimmed with a tangle of logs, beached giants tossed bleached and barren on to the shore.

'Driftwood,' she murmured with some surprise. She had held a hazy picture of driftwood being small, well shaped pieces of wood that people collected for crafts. She stepped on one half buried log and, deciding that for the most part they were securely balanced, began to step from one to another, jumping quickly down the beach.

Soon tired, but feeling much more relaxed, she stopped and leaned against one log, facing the ocean. Closing her eyes, she tilted her head and took a deep breath, testing the salty tang in the air. With a sigh of pleasure, she reached up and pulled the pins from her hair, releasing it to the wind. 'Oh, this is perfect!'

Grinning, she left the logs and started towards the water. The stretch of sand from the logs to the water was surprisingly wide, and she ran until she came to the edge of the ocean, tiny waves lapping the soles of her boots. The real waves broke off-shore, scattering silver-grey spray high in the air.

Stefanie continued walking, stopping to examine bits of shell and seaweed, heading vaguely towards a large black rock not too far distant. She stepped agilely over the rivulets of water that trickled between her and the rock. Her long legs took the jagged slope with ease, and when she reached the top she turned and looked down the beach of packed creamy sand, broken only by scattered circlets of black rock, similar to the one on which she stood. Inland she could see misty blue mountains still covered with snow, and all around were the giant evergreen trees of cedar, hemlock and Douglas fir.

It may be spring, but it's not that warm yet, Stefanie realised with a shiver, and zipped up the collar of her jacket. But who cares? It's bright and sunny and I feel better than I have in a long time! With that last thought she scampered over the rock to the sea side, smiling happily. The ocean was a new experience to her and she was determined to become as familiar with it as she was with the windswept prairies she had just left. She found a sheltered nook and settled against the sunwarmed rock, her eyes never leaving the waves that broke below, mesmerising her with their endless rhythm.

How I wish Dad was here to share this with me, she

thought, longing for the companionship the two of
them had shared. No one had yet come close to filling
the lonely gap his death two years ago had left in her
life. Theirs had been a close relationship.

When his wife had died tragically at the age of
twenty-nine, David Hart had packed up his small
daughter and moved from Toronto to work for a
mining company in northern Manitoba. The Canadian
Shield is rich in minerals and ores, and he sought them,
finding places for his company to open new mines.
Stefanie had accompanied her father everywhere. He
refused to leave her in the care of strangers, and she
spent her childhood in surveyors' camps, learning first-
hand the splendours of the great Canadian north.

Her father's contemporaries, at first taken aback by
this distinctly feminine addition to their masculine
crews, soon succumbed to the curly red-headed tot with
the sparkling green eyes. Stefanie had it made. She had
a kind and caring father and an over-abundance of
doting 'uncles'. She learned the elementary aspects of
geology from Uncle Rick and basic French from Oncle
André. Uncle Ian taught her how to set up a proper
bush camp and to bake bannock over the coals of a
campfire, while Uncle Tom insisted she learn how to
clean the lake trout and pickeral he taught her to catch.

The list was endless. Men came and went each year,
each offering his particular brand of friendship to the
little girl. They gave her the affection they might have
offered the daughters or little sisters left behind in some
southern section of the vast country.

The last carefree time she spent in the endless days of
a northern summer came when she was fifteen. She had
stopped calling most of the men Uncle by then, but still
tagged along in little girl fashion whenever she could.
She had grown rapidly during the past winter and was
almost her full adult height. Her bright red hair had
deepened to a dark auburn and most of the stubborn
freckles had faded from her short straight nose. She was
a pretty girl on the verge of becoming a beautiful
woman—a fact that had not escaped the notice of a
new man in camp.

No one realised that Frank Dawson's avuncular attentions were really the basis of a well planned seduction. A seduction that to Stefanie's lasting horror became ugly and violent when she tried to refuse him. Her father had arrived back in camp unexpectedly, and had pulled his shocked and sobbing daughter from Dawson's lustful embrace. The scene that followed was ferocious. Stefanie watched in terror as her father nearly killed the other man. It was only the intervention of the other men arriving back in camp that had prevented him from facing a possible manslaughter charge.

The attack had done one thing. It had awakened David Hart to the fact that his daughter was no longer a little girl. He was forced to realise the unsuitability and isolation of the life she was leading. Because there was no other choice, he sent her to a girls' school in the south of the province.

Still badly frightened and missing her father more than she had ever thought possible, Stefanie tried desperately to fit into a schoolgirl's life. Most of her education to this point had been correspondence lessons learned at her father's knee. The formality of the classes and the relative lack of freedom to explore new thoughts and ideas frustrated her almost as much as her inability to fit into the life of a normal fifteen-year-old girl. Things such as make-up and boy talk were as alien to her as the city in which she was confined. Many a lonely night she sobbed out her frustrations and fears into the pillow of the narrow cot in a room she shared with three other girls.

Gradually the strangeness had abated. With her well trained mind and free thinking she found herself at the top of her class as often as not, and she began to enjoy the friendly competition with the other girls. Class outings to the symphony and ballet enchanted her. When her father came to visit, they explored the city until it was as familiar and friendly to her as the lakes and rivers of the north had been.

Stefanie led her class at graduation, and her father had settled her and her best friend into a tiny apartment near the university. She aimed towards a commerce degree and entered happily into the life of a university student. She had no worries—her father was able to meet all her expenses. Studies, parties and long talks until dawn filled the next four years.

Stefanie smiled, still lost in the memory of those university days. It had been fun—hard work, but fun. She stretched against her backrest of stone and yawned hugely. Relaxed now, she began to feel the first stirrings of hunger. It was a long time since the bowl of clam chowder she had enjoyed in Port Alberni before starting the last leg of her trip. She yawned again and stood up, shivering in the blast of cold wind that hit her as soon as she left the shelter of the rock. Clouds were starting to cover the blue sky, and she pulled her jacket tighter around her and turned to go.

The wind was stronger than it had been before and the waves crashed with more force and reach. Stefanie walked quickly over the top of the rock, already anticipating a good meal and, later, a fire. But first, she thought with a grimace, I've got to unload the car!

She stopped abruptly, and stared with growing horror. Where before there had been mere inches of water between the rock and shore, there was now a good twelve feet of surf. Restless seeking water, turbulent in its desire to claim the beach. Stefanie moaned with a mixed feeling of despair and anger. 'How could I have been so stupid!' she chastised herself, scrambling down to stand on the lowermost rocky ridge where the water broke on its inward flow.

She stood there, cursing aloud at her stupidity. Ignorance of the ocean's ways was no real excuse for this predicament. Now what am I going to do? she wondered. Stay here or swim? How long does it take for the tide to change anyway? Not knowing just what to do, she stood staring down into the water.

'I would advise you to start wading before you have to swim.'

Stefanie jumped at the unexpected voice commanding her from across the widening gap. She struggled to keep her balance on the slippery rock and stared, still silent, at the man standing where she wanted to be.

'I said,' he repeated, 'start wading!' He stood, arms crossed imperiously, bearded chin thrust forward.

Stefanie stiffened with anger. 'Couldn't you get a boat or something?' she shouted back crossly, making no attempt to move.

'By the time I could get a boat—or something—back here, there'll be several more feet of water between you and the shore. And the turbulence around those rocks is more than I care to contend with. We'd be swamped. I have no intention of getting wet.' Stefanie could hear the sarcasm in his voice even across the expanse of rushing water.

Frowning, she quickly removed her jacket and sat down to untie her boots. No point in soaking these, she thought, and sighed with impatience when the wet leather lace slipped into a tight knot. Great, she muttered as she struggled with the reluctant knot, sneaking a quick glance at the man on the beach. Why doesn't he go home? She would much rather make the crossing without an audience, but the stranger showed no signs of leaving. In fact, he seemed to be settling down to wait.

'Better hurry,' he called, 'or you'll be getting more than the seat of your pants wet!'

Damn the man! Stefanie cursed under her breath until at last the knot untied. She was more than tempted to ignore him, to march right back to the other side of the rock, but she resisted the urge, not knowing just how long she would have to wait until the tide went out again. The idea of spending several cold hungry hours perched on a rock in the middle of the ocean appealed to her even less than what she had to do now. She tied the boots together, slung them over her shoulder, took a deep breath and gingerly lowered herself into the water.

The cold was instantly numbing. The water crept past her knees, her thighs, right up to her waist. It was a struggle to keep her balance. The current was strong and the waves ploughed around her, soaking her back and shoulders with an iciness that would have rivalled any Arctic water. Stefanie's mind was almost as numb as her body when she staggered to the dry sand and stood dripping and shivering in front of the stranger.

'Y-you could have helped!' She was angry and uncomfortable.

He raised one dark eyebrow and stared down at her. 'You were managing quite well by yourself,' he said, 'and I could see no reason why I should get wet because of your stupidity.'

'I-It wasn't stupidity!' Stefanie forced the words out through chattering teeth. 'I forgot the time. S-so I would have been stranded f-for a bit. S-so what?'

He stared at her with narrowed grey eyes, their expression as cold as the water she had just left. 'Stupidity,' he repeated bitingly. 'That bit, as you put it, would have been several hours, during which time the water would have reached the top of the rocks. The chances are you would have been swept out to sea with the first big wave. People drown in these waters every year.'

He bent down to pick up the pack he had laid on the sand. 'Now, if you're through with your little snit, I suggest you put on that dry jacket.' His cold grey eyes swept over her with no softening in their expression. 'You look—frozen.' His gaze lingered on her breasts, peaked with cold and moulded tightly by the semi-transparency of her wet T-shirt. With a contemptuous smile at her start of embarrassment, he hefted the pack on to his broad back, turned on his heel and strode off without a backward glance.

Stefanie, her coldness forgotten in the fury that rushed over her at his rudeness, searched wildly for something to hurl at the retreating figure. Finding nothing, she stamped her stockinged foot on the soft sand and sputtered with impotent rage. Suddenly icy, she struggled into the warmth of her jacket, picked up her boots, and ran back to the house.

When she reached the car, she fumbled with numbed fingers for the keys she had put in her jacket pocket. For one heart-stopping moment she thought they had fallen out, but thankfully her fingers finally closed over them. With shaking hands she opened the boot and grabbed a suitcase, let the cat out and hurried to the back door of the house, desperate for warmth.

She unlocked the door and stepped into the kitchen. She started stripping off her clothes as soon as the door shut behind her, leaving them in a sodden heap on the red brick floor. A hasty search through the suitcase found a long velour robe, and she gratefully enveloped her shivering body in its thick folds. Only then did she manage enough interest in her surroundings to look around.

It was a pretty kitchen. The cupboards were painted a soft white with patterns of tiny blue flowers around the corners. There was a large window looking out over the tree-filled yard. Under the window was a large table of warm maple brown. And best of all, she decided as she looked around, was the very modern dishwasher built into the counter next to the sink.

A white louvred door separated the kitchen from the rest of the house. Stefanie pushed through it, still trembling with the cold that seemed, if possible, to be getting worse. She looked around the living room and managed a pleased smile. It wasn't going to be hard to live here for the next few weeks. Crossing the shiny wooden floor, she drew aside the coppery-coloured curtains to reveal a whole wall of floor-to-ceiling windows through which she could catch glimpses of the ocean between towering trees.

Quivering with cold, she turned away from the window. Before she explored any further, she needed a bath. With lots and lots of hot water, she thought with growing urgency. There was a tiny circular staircase in the corner of the room leading to what had to be the bedroom. And where there's a bedroom, Stefanie thought as she quickly climbed the stairs, there's usually a bathroom!

The bedroom was really a loft. As she stood at the foot of the wide bed she could see past the railing out over the living room to the ocean beyond. There was a walk-in closet on one side of the room, and on the other, at last, the bathroom. It was tiny, but pretty, with green fixtures and wallpaper patterned with sprigged blossoms.

A very audible sigh of relief lingered in the air as Stefanie slid into the steamy warmth of the bath. She closed her eyes thankfully as she felt the chill leave her body, and added more water until it was as hot as she could stand it. The partially closed door pushed open and the cat trotted in. He stood on his hind legs and peered into the tub. Reaching with one big black paw, he patted the water delicately and questioned her with an anxious mew.

'It's okay, puss,' Stefanie assured him, scratching his chin with a languid hand. 'But if you ever see a man with a bristly black beard wandering around—bite!' Her humour was returning fast as the chill left her.

It was careless, she had to acknowledge, but I doubt if it was as bad as he made out. What a rude arrogant man! She felt anger stirring again and sat up suddenly reaching for the soap. She washed herself vigorously, trying to dispel the picture of contemptuous grey eyes lingering on her wet body. Damn the man! she cursed, slipping beneath the water once more with more force than necessary. She swore again, more soundly this time as water slopped over the side of the tub, soaking the floor and the cat, who stalked out of the room with his ears laid back and wet tail dragging.

Much later, wrapped in her thick green housecoat, Stefanie curled up in front of the fire. The fireplace was huge and the area directly in front was sunk lower than the rest of the living room. It was covered with a rich rug of cream, shot with yellows and browns, and the entire area was filled with soft sheepskins and cushions of every size and colour imaginable. A regular passion pit, Stefanie had decided with a grin. She sighed with pleasure, sipping the dry red wine she had poured herself after supper. The cat, as close to the source of heat as he could get without scorching, lay stretched out full length, sound asleep.

Stefanie twirled the wine glass between her fingers, staring into the ruby liquid. She should have been exhausted after the long drive and her reluctant baptism in the icy brine, but even the combined warmth of fire and wine couldn't still her thoughts. Perhaps it was the time spent reminiscing about her father that had begun this dredge of old memories—no, not old memories. Tony . . .

No! She would not think of Tony, not tonight. With unnecessary force, Stefanie set her glass on the stone hearth. Would she ever get over the hurt of Tony's betrayal? Yes! she told herself firmly. Now that she had made the break, with a new job to start and new friends to be found, it was just a matter of time. Just a little more time.

Determined to stop the flow of thought before it became the night's obsession, Stefanie got up quickly and climbed the tiny flight of stairs to the bedroom. She unzipped her robe, letting it fall into a heap on the floor. She buttoned up a man's flannel shirt, worn thin by many washings, pulled on a pair of faded denim overalls and thick woollen socks. Thankful that she had at least managed to keep her boots dry this afternoon, she pulled them on and laced them tight. Reaching for a windbreaker, she ran downstairs, gave the cat an absentminded pat and went out of the door.

The wind hit her, damp with salty spray and lingering rain. She tied the hood of her jacket tighter, rammed her hands into her pockets and walked determinedly towards the beach. She clambered over drift logs left slippery by the driving rain of late afternoon, and stood on one giant nearest the shore. To her surprise, the water that this afternoon had lapped at the sand some two hundred yards from the logs now surged inches from where she stood.

With a sense of foreboding, Stefanie turned and, balancing on the precarious logs, made her way down the beach in the direction she had taken that afternoon. She reached the point where she was sure she had left the logs attracted by the rock—but there was no rock to be seen. Even in the uncertain light, she could see nothing but turbulent water, rolling and twisting in, spitting up at her feet.

She sat down with a violent shiver. So, she thought, he was right. She shook her head in disbelief. It just didn't seem possible that there could be such a difference between low and high tide. Would she have stayed there until the water went down? Stefanie didn't know. She just felt an overwhelming thankfulness that all she had suffered was a cold dunking. It could have been so much worse. She stood up and started walking on the strip of sand left between the logs and the water. I guess I owe him an apology, she thought, and then, remembering the cold grey eyes, decided thankfully that she would probably never see him again.

She continued walking, her senses sharpened and aware in the dark night. It was beginning to clear somewhat, and occasional clouds would be ripped back by the wind to reveal a fleeting glimpse of stars. The narrow strip of sand she was confined to was slowly becoming wider, but the steady and relentless wind continued to push the water to her feet.

Just about to turn and head back, she caught a glimpse of light through the trees. Neighbours! she thought with delight. Night had shown her just how remote and devoid of human companionship this area was. Curious, she stepped carefully over the logs and picked her way towards the source of the light. Hidden among the trees was a house, light streaming from a large picture window. Stefanie could see a man sitting at a table near the window, a typewriter in front of him with papers piled around it. Not wanting to spy on anyone, she was about to turn for home when the man stood up.

It's him! she realised with a start. Intrigued, she stayed where she was and watched while the man of that afternoon threw another log on the fire. He returned to his chair and sat stroking his beard while he stared at his typewriter. With a quick movement he leaned forward to rip a piece of paper from the carriage, crumple it up and then throw it down. From the look on his face Stefanie figured it was joining a growing pile.

Good! She grinned in the dark. I hope he's stuck! He

might have been right about her predicament this afternoon, but his manner had been inexcusably rude. And then, with a suddenness that startled her, he stood up, flicked off the light and walked towards a dimmer glow at the rear of the house. Stefanie stumbled in the darkness, grabbing on to a tree trunk to steady herself. Conscious of the surrounding blackness and the chill that was slowly invading her body, she shivered and with a strong sense of isolation, began to retrace her steps.

CHAPTER TWO

THERE was a weight on her chest, a heaviness that wouldn't go away. Stefanie struggled to take a breath, moaning in her sleep, fighting, trying to turn. Her eyes opened and she stared unseeing into two glowing yellow orbs. For a moment she fought with panic, and then, as reality finally dawned, she groaned loudly and thrust the heavy black cat from her chest.

'Honestly, you miserable beast, I swear I'm going to rent you a room in a dog pound! Let me sleep!' She rolled over, pulled the covers under her chin and snuggled down to sleep. The cat was having none of it. He wanted out. He sat beside her pillow gently batting her cheek with one giant forepaw until, in exasperation, she threw back the covers to stumble out of bed and down the stairs. Muttering under her breath, she opened the door to the eager animal, shuddered as the sullen grey rain touched her bare skin and quickly retraced her steps. She fell on to the bed and with a contented sigh burrowed beneath the covers once more. Maybe I'll get up some time tomorrow, she thought with a yawn, and was instantly asleep.

Next time it was a pounding noise that woke her, a heavy knocking that conveyed a message of urgency. Pulling her robe around her, Stefanie stumbled down the stairs once more to the back door. She flung it open and stood there smothering a yawn, her eyes heavy with sleep, her hair a glorious tumble of red curls.

'Yes?' she asked, and then stepped back, her eyes widening in alarm. 'You!' she whispered, looking into cold grey eyes framed by dark beard and gold-tipped curls.

'Me,' he returned mockingly. 'This, I assume, is yours.' He thrust a squirming black bundle at her.

Stefanie took it, startled, and asked with quick concern, 'What happened? Is he all right?'

24

'He's just fine—which is more than I can say for the birds he's been after all morning! I was tempted to tie a brick to his tail and drop him off the end of the wharf, but decided to do the neighbourly thing and give him one more chance. I might have known he'd belong to you.'

Stefanie winced at the sarcasm in his voice. 'I—I'm sorry,' she managed, then gasped as the cat took a sudden leap to the floor. His hind leg caught in the vee of her robe and pulled it open to expose a creamy swell of breast. She flushed with embarrassment when the stranger's cold look softened with momentary interest. She stepped back and pulled the robe tight over her bare skin, suddenly aware of how foolish she was to open the door so easily to a stranger. He was looking at her fully now, with a derisive smile as if aware exactly what she was thinking. Stefanie looked wildly about for some means of protection.

'Don't panic,' he said sardonically. 'I've got other things on my mind this morning. Besides,' he continued, letting his eyes roam over her, 'I don't go for little girls—no matter how precocious.'

'Oh, go away,' Stefanie muttered crossly.

'I'm going, little girl,' he said, 'but keep that animal away from my place or I'll be back.' With one last look that lingered on her pale face and huge green eyes, he turned and walked away with long strides.

Stefanie shut the door and leaned against it, relieved that he had gone. 'Thanks a lot, Pete,' she muttered to the cat who was crouched down in front of his food dish. 'I could have been attacked right here in my own kitchen and you wouldn't have raised a paw in my defence—you even drag 'em home! I'm going to trade you in for a dog!' She stood in the middle of the room rubbing her forehead in exasperation. There was no going back to sleep now, which was just as well considering it was almost eleven o'clock. With a shrug, she put all thought of the dark stranger from her mind. No man was going to ruin her holiday!

She began to rummage through unpacked boxes of groceries for coffee. Fortunately, the house came fully equipped and she found an up-to-date coffee-maker in one of the cupboards. While the coffee was brewing she foraged in the fridge for breakfast. Soon she sat down to a plate of crisp bacon, scrambled eggs and golden hash brown potatoes. By the time she had finished, she had polished off not only the plateful of food and potful of coffee, but toast and jam as well.

Stefanie found food a joy, a sensuous experience, both the preparation and the eating. It was the cleaning up afterwards that she hated. She pushed back her chair from the table, looked around the kitchen with a grimace, remembered the dishwasher and brightened somewhat. It helped.

When the dishes were stacked in the dishwasher, the boxes unpacked and the rest of the kitchen tidied, Stefanie went upstairs to dress. She pulled on the faded overalls and worn shirt of last night. After four years of dressing carefully for the office every morning, she was ready for a break. No make-up and the easiest of hairstyles, she decided, and quickly plaited her hair into two long French braids.

Now what do I do? she wondered after she had made the bed. She felt too energetic to just sit and read, although it was a perfect day for it. She wandered into the living room and opened the curtains. It was still gloomy, the clouds lying thick and low over the grey ocean. She had just decided to take a walk regardless of the weather conditions, when she caught a glimpse of a solitary figure making its way down the shore.

'Him again!' Stefanie muttered, and knew she didn't want to risk another encounter just yet. The cold arrogance of the man disturbed her. 'I should have known this place sounded too good to be true,' she said to the cat. 'No one said anything about having to put up with miserable neighbours!' She brightened. 'I know—I'll make a pie.' It was a good rainy day activity and she cheered at the thought of a golden apple pie bubbling with spices and brown sugar.

It didn't take long to make. She had made so many over the years that she had it down to a routine. She quickly rolled out the pastry and fitted it into a pie plate. That done, she pared the apples, cut them into a bowl, added a generous sprinkling of nutmeg and cinnamon, mixed in the sugar and filled the pie plate to the rim. She dotted the mixture with butter, rolled over the top pastry and deftly trimmed it to fit. She popped it into the oven and gave a sigh of satisfaction that quickly turned into a groan of despair when she surveyed the mess she had made.

'What a disaster!' she exclaimed with disgust, and dug in. She stacked bowls, wiped counter tops and swept crumbs of dough from the red brick floor. 'There, that's it for the day. I'll make sandwiches for supper!'

The cat, just awakened from another prolonged nap, yawned, raised a hind leg straight in the air and began to clean himself vigorously. Finally satisfied, he walked over to the door and stood, nose to the crack, waiting to be noticed. Laughing, Stefanie reached for her jacket. 'Hang on, puss,' she said. 'I'll join you.'

The two of them stepped out into the cool gray day. No rude stuck-up man is going to confine me to the house, she vowed as she followed the path to the beach. This place is big enough for me and six others like him—I'll just make sure to stay away from him. All the same, she was glad to see no other person on the beach.

Unconsciously she chose the direction she had taken yesterday, walking close to the water. The cat trotted beside her, his thick black tail held erect as he carefully avoided the incoming waves. Stefanie walked slowly with her head down, searching the sand for treasures, pocketing the occasional pretty shell.

She hadn't gone far when she noticed the cat was no longer with her. Quickly looking around, she caught sight of him just as he disappeared over the logs, heading straight for a house hidden in the trees. Stefanie grimaced when she realised that it had to be the same place she had seen last night—his place. Breaking into an easy run, she followed the path her cat had taken. Maybe, she thought hopefully, he isn't home, and then as she neared the house and heard a clamour of squawking birds, rolled her eyes upward and prayed he wasn't.

She rounded the corner of the house to the backyard and stopped. Just off the house was a large pen full of ducks, geese and seagulls, milling around, trying to escape the big black cat crouched low and stalking. Before she could do more than take a step forward, the man came quietly from the house with a bucket in his hands. He walked up to the cat and calmly dumped the contents over it. Without a sound, the cat was gone, a dripping black streak tearing through the bush.

For a moment Stefanie was highly indignant at the treatment of her pet, but she quickly realised that a bucket of water would do Pete less harm than would his continued presence around the penned birds. She turned to leave before she was seen, but something in the sound of the man's rich chuckle as he stood arms akimbo, looking in the direction the cat had taken, stopped her. Folding her arms against her chest, she leaned against the corner of the house, her own sense of humour breaking through.

'You can rest easy,' she said, her voice low with amusement. 'He won't be back.'

The man whirled around, surprise wiping the grin from his face. He stared at her for a moment, running his hand through a thick tangle of curls, his eyes somewhat perplexed. 'It was just water,' he said with a note of apology in his deep voice. 'These birds are wild—most of them are recovering from some sort of injury and shouldn't be disturbed,' he went on to explain. 'And there just aren't many ways to discourage a cat intent on the hunt.'

'Other than tying bricks to their tails?' Stefanie was careful to keep her voice light and unaccusing.

'Ah, yes, I guess I was a bit—abrupt this morning.'

Stefanie inclined her head with a slight smile. 'A bit,' she agreed airily. She didn't want to antagonise him further. If they were going to be neighbours for the next few weeks, they could at least be civil. If she was honest she would have to admit that it was her fault they had got off to a bad start, and Pete certainly hadn't helped matters with his sudden desire to add hunting to his list of misdemeanours. Reacting instinctively, she stepped forward. 'I'm Stefanie Hart,' she introduced herself, and held out her hand with the ease of one used to shaking hands.

'And I'm Jesse Stuart,' he said with a quizzical smile and briefly enclosed her slender hand in his big warm one.

Stefanie studied him warily, but saw none of the arrogance that had irritated her earlier. His grey eyes exuded a vibrant warmth as they returned her study and she felt a spurt of relief, knowing she wouldn't have to spend her holidays trying to avoid an irate neighbour after all.

Impulsively she walked over to the pen and crouched down, peering through the wire. 'Have all these birds been hurt?' There weren't nearly as many as all the commotion had led her to believe.

'No,' he replied, coming over to squat down beside her. 'The Canada geese are a mated pair.' He pointed at two big geese watching cautiously from a far corner, eyes bright with intelligence. 'The male has an injured wing—gunshot, I think. The female could leave any time but chooses to stay with him. Canada geese mate for life, have even been known to give their lives for each other.' He ended with a short laugh.

Stefanie shot him a glance from the corners of her eyes. That laugh seemed out of place—had there been an undercurrent of bitterness there, as though he was relating the loyalty of the birds to his own life? Curious about the man kneeling beside her, she watched him covertly while he talked informatively about the other birds.

'That,' he continued unaware of her scrutiny, 'is Charlie.' As he pointed the gull threw its head back emitting a string of raucous calls. 'He stays for the free grub.'

Stefanie laughed as she watched the bird's antics. 'He sounds like he's starving to death! What do you feed them?'

'Mainly grains for the geese and ducks,' he answered with a smile that seemed impossibly warm after the coldness she had seen earlier. 'Charlie'll gulp down anything that doesn't run faster than he does.' He pointed to a burlap sack leaning against a tree that formed one of the posts of the pen. 'Throw some feed in for them—it'll calm them down after that attack by your vicious animal.'

Stefanie quickly complied, feeling guilty. 'He isn't really,' she said, tossing grain over the top of the wire pen. 'He's never even nabbed a sparrow before. Charlie would have been too much for him.' She watched with amusement as the gull pushed its greedy way past the other birds to be at the head of the handout. She wiped her hands on her jeans and turned to smile politely. 'Thanks for showing me the birds,' she said warmly. 'I should be going now.'

'Wait—er—Stefanie,' he said, stroking his glossy black beard. 'I was about to make some coffee when I saw your animal about to snack on my birds. Would you like some—with doughnuts?'

Stefanie hesitated. The invitation seemed sincere enough and it was certainly the neighbourly thing to do. Why not? she thought. 'Okay,' she accepted with a smile, and then stopped, a look of concern on her face. 'What time is it?'

He looked puzzled as he glanced at his watch. 'Three-twenty. Why?'

'I left a pie in the oven,' she replied. 'And it was done five minutes ago! I'll have to take a raincheck—unless,' she added impulsively, 'you would like to come over to my place for the coffee and hot apple pie?'

'I can't resist,' he admitted with a grin. 'Go ahead—I'll follow in a couple of minutes.'

Stefanie was off and running, hoping she wouldn't find a charred mess waiting for her. She ran gasping into the kitchen, opened the oven door and pulled out a golden-brown pie.

'Perfect!' She placed it on the counter to cool. Slipping out of her jacket, she ran upstairs to smooth her hair and splash cold water on her flushed face, thinking about the man—Jesse. She frowned slightly. Had she been too hasty in inviting him over? Somehow she didn't think so. Surely a man who so

carefully tended to the needs of injured birds couldn't
be that bad, and his manner towards her had
certainly warmed since this morning. With a shrug,
she went down to make the coffee. She would just
have to wait and see.

The coffee had just finished brewing when he arrived.
For a moment Stefanie thought the arrogance of earlier
was back, but then, with relief, she saw that his eyes
were a warm grey. He took a deep breath of the spicy
aroma lingering in the air and grinned at her. 'The smell
alone beats the doughnuts I had in mind hands down,'
he admitted.

'Wait till you taste it,' Stefanie said confidently,
putting a generous wedge on the table. 'Sit down,' she
added, and poured steaming coffee into the waiting
mugs.

Jesse folded his long legs under the table and picked
up his fork. 'Perfect,' he stated a moment later around a
mouthful of flaky crust.

'Thanks,' Stefanie smiled, and nibbled her own
portion.

There was a short silence as though they were both
searching for something to say. He spoke first. 'I see
you're from Manitoba.'

Stefanie looked up, startled. 'How did you know?'

'Licence plates,' he responded promptly. 'Have you
been out here long?'

'Just over a week,' she replied. 'I stayed in Vancouver
for a week.'

'And your parents—will they be joining you?'

'My parents?' Surely she didn't look that young? She
was just about to set him straight when she had a
sudden vision of his face as he had looked at her this
morning and with a barely concealed shudder,
remembered how they had lingered on her exposed
skin. 'Oh, they—they couldn't make it at the last
minute,' she invented without hesitation. 'D-Daddy had
some business problem.' She shrugged as though her
father's business was of little concern to her. 'Too bad,'
she continued to fabricate. 'It would have been their
first stay on the coast.' What am I doing? she asked

herself with dismay as she heard the lies trip effortlessly off her tongue.

Jesse noticed nothing. 'Then this must be your first visit—although it seemed rather obvious yesterday.' He looked at her suddenly, a frown marking his forehead.

Stefanie was uncomfortable, wishing he hadn't brought it up. 'Yes, well—I guess it was a stupid thing to do.'

'Stupid and dangerous,' he agreed, not making any allowances.

She sat quietly, an embarrassed flush staining her cheeks. After last night she was all too aware that she deserved the censure she could hear in his voice. To her surprise, he reached across the table and touched her clenched hand with gentle fingers.

'Hey, Stefanie, I'm not rubbing it in—honest. It's just that . . .' He stopped, a shadowed look touching his face. 'There was a girl last summer, did much the same thing as you did yesterday. She was sixteen—not that much younger than you. Probably just as pretty too, although it was hard to tell.' His face hardened. 'We found her two days after she went missing, floating face down in a tidal pool. The only thing recognisable was her hair.' He reached out and touched a ruby plait. 'It was long and red—just like yours.'

Stefanie closed her eyes in horror. 'No wonder you were so angry yesterday! I—I'm sorry.'

'Just make sure you don't do it again,' he said severely, then flashed her a wide smile. 'Now, could I have some more coffee? It's really quite good.'

'Sure can.' Sensing that he would say no more about her blunder, Stefanie jumped up and poured him another cup. 'Would you like some more pie? There's lots.'

'Yes, please,' he said promptly, and handed her his plate.

Stefanie studied him while he ate. He really does think I'm a kid, she thought, but it wasn't too surprising. She had found early in her career that without careful attention to make-up and clothing styles, no one would take her seriously. It was somewhat disconcerting to realise that he didn't seem to think she wasn't much more than seventeen or eighteen, however, and she started to tell him the truth, but something held the words back. Let him think she was a teenager. It might just be—safer.

'Are you on holiday too,' Mr Stuart?' she asked ingenuously.

He looked at her, slightly surprised. Maybe it was her use of his surname. 'No—no, I'm here to write a booklet for the government. Sort of an introduction to the park. Pacific Rim attracts people from all over Canada and the States. Most of them have never been near the ocean before—except for a stroll around English Bay in the heart of downtown Vancouver. Yes, Stefanie,' he said with a smile, 'people just like you. I plan to include a brief history, descriptions of the plant and animal life—that sort of thing.'

'Gee, Mr Stuart,' Stefanie said, slipping easily into the role she had decided to play, 'that sounds exactly like what I need. I wish it was already written.' She managed to sound very young and slightly wistful.

'Well, Stefanie,' Jesse drawled as he stood up to leave, 'maybe I'll let you tag along with me one of these days. Consider it payment for the delicious pie.'

'Hey, that would be great! Thanks, Mr Stuart.' Stefanie barely managed to keep from smirking. Really, this was too easy! With a wave of his hand, Jesse was gone, striding rapidly through the trees in the direction of his house. Stefanie leaned in the doorway watching until he was out of sight, a bemused smile on her face. 'Goodbye, Mr Stuart,' she said out loud, and giggled, her mood buoyant as she shut the door.

Later, as she passed by the full-length mirror in the bedroom, she stopped and looked closely at herself. No wonder he thinks I'm seventeen, she laughed. Look at me! Two long red braids hung to her shoulders, which were covered with a checked flannel shirt, which was in turn covered by faded denim overalls, below which peeped two tiny feet encased in fuzzy woollen socks. Seven persistent freckles marched across her nose and her eyes were round and soft, completely free of the make-up that would have made her look closer to her actual age.

'Yep,' she said ruefully, 'that's seventeen!' She turned away unable to see that it was not just the overalls or braids, but the air of innocence that she wore around her like a rare perfume that more than anything gave her a youthful appearance.

Stefanie lit the fire just as it began to grow dark. The cat had returned shortly before, extremely indignant. 'Better stay away from him, Pete,' she advised. 'He's not a man to fool with!' She shrugged off the feeling that maybe she should heed the warning herself, laughing at the cat as he furiously tried to restore order to his damp fur.

Feeling a little bit sorry for him—after all, a cat did have strong instincts for hunting—she gave him a generous serving of raw hamburger for his supper. Somewhat mollified by this treat, he allowed himself to be brushed and petted until he fell asleep, curled up in front of a roaring blaze.

Stefanie was more content this evening as well. She soaked long and luxuriously in a bubble bath, sipping a glass of cold white wine while reading an exciting bestseller. It was only when she realised that the fire would surely die unless it was refuelled that she left the water, dried and stepped into her robe. She refilled her glass, carried it into the living room and threw more logs on the fire before leaning back on a pile of cushions with her book.

It wasn't long before her eyelids fluttered shut and the book slipped from her slackened fingers. With a tiny murmur she turned on the cushion to face the fire and slept.

She dreamt, a confusing puzzle of pictures swirling before her mind's eye. She could hear Tony's taunts of frigid! frigid! coming from Frank Dawson's lips as he pulled her hair in a cruel grip and bent to kiss her. She struggled, defiant and helpless, but when his lips touched hers she saw not Dawson's lust-crazed eyes, but cold grey ones, framed by black beard and gold-tipped curls. And then suddenly she stood alone, dripping wet and icy cold, on an endless stretch of dark beach.

Her eyes opened as suddenly as they had closed, chasing away the disturbing images. She stared unseeing into the dying fire until the growing chill began to penetrate her prone figure. Still trance-like, she crawled over and threw another log on the fire, then sat hypnotised as it blazed into flame. She hugged her knees against her chest, feeling a heavy depression settle over her. Tony's accusations about her sexuality rang closer to the truth than perhaps he really knew. There had never been even one man she had desired as a lover, not even Tony—not really. There had never been even one kiss that had left her feeling anything but cold and uncomfortable.

Stefanie sighed. Maybe it would be better to be like some women she knew, able to take love whenever it came, whether it lasted for one night or ten. Why had she never felt anything for any of the men she had known? Who was she waiting for? There was no Prince Charming waiting in the wings to come charging out on his white horse to rescue her from a love-starved existence. Would she ever have the needs and desires of a normal woman? It was beginning to look hopeless.

Stefanie felt even more depressed by her thoughts. Maybe I shouldn't have come here, she thought bitterly. Maybe I needed bright lights and lots of people— distractions rather than time to brood. She got up slowly to throw a last log on the fire. 'C'mon, Pete,' she said, picking up the sleeping animal and starting towards the stairs. 'I need a teddy bear tonight.' She rubbed her cheek on his soft fur and went to her lonely bed.

CHAPTER THREE

THE first thing Stefanie saw the next morning was the sun. It streamed bright light through the tiny window cut into the sloping ceiling above her bed and fell into a golden puddle on the blankets beside her. With a sense of anticipation, she pushed back the covers, grabbed her robe and ran down the stairs, pausing in the living room to open the curtains. The sky was clear and blue, right over the ocean.

'Perfect!' She danced into the kitchen to make coffee. She opened the back door for the cat and took a deep breath of the clear air full of the aroma of cedar mingled with brine. Smiling to herself and feeling so much better after last night's unaccountable depression, she returned to the kitchen to prepare breakfast.

After an enjoyable and leisurely meal, she dressed quickly in cream-coloured cords and an emerald green sweater. She braided her hair and went downstairs to put on her boots and jacket. She had wasted enough time indoors.

The beach was deserted, the tide way out. As she was walking along the water mark, she heard a shout from behind, and turned to see Jesse emerging from the trees along the shore. He waved and beckoned to her. Smiling, she started to walk towards him. She would enjoy the company.

'Stefanie,' he greeted. 'You're up early today.'

'It was the sun,' she said with a smile. 'Isn't it a beautiful day?'

'It's perfect,' he agreed. 'Especially for the pictures I want to take, and the tide is just right. Want to come?'

'Sure—where are you going?' Stefanie fell into step beside him.

'Those rocks over there,' he replied, pointing about half a mile down the beach in the opposite direction to the one she had taken before. 'There are some very pretty tidal pools over there, lots of anemones and starfish. I should get some good pictures.'

Stefanie found herself sneaking quick glances at him as they walked down the beach. He was considerably taller than she was, something that didn't happen very often. He was handsome too, she decided after a furtive look at his strong profile. His hair was a tangle of dark, almost black curls, the ends of which looked as though they had been bleached by last summer's sun. Gold-tipped, she had called it, and decided after another look that it looked quite attractive when combined with his glossy black beard.

He turned suddenly when they neared the rocks. 'Now,' he said, 'if you watch the waves you'll see that the tide is still going out. We've got lots of time before it turns.'

Stefanie smiled to herself, as she followed him. The lessons had started. What had looked to her like a cluster of several big black rocks was really one large much worn mass. In between the craggy protrusions were crystal pools of ocean left by the retreating tide. Jesse led the way to one of the larger ones and dropped the pack he was carrying.

'Look,' he said, kneeling beside the water. 'See those white shells on the rock? They're barnacles.' He grabbed her hand and pulled her down beside him. 'Now, look at the ones still covered with water—see that little frond waving from the top? Look close.'

Carefully withdrawing her hand from his warm grip, Stefanie knelt down closer to the water and peered below the surface. After a moment she could see tiny brown feathers fanning the water. 'I see them—what are they?'

'The cirri—feet. The barnacle combs the water with it looking for particles of food.' He looked at her with a grin. 'The barnacle has been described as an animal that sits on its head and kicks food into its mouth.'

Stefanie's delighted laughter rang in the air. 'I like that,' she said, flashing him a grin of genuine pleasure. She bent back down and continued to examine the minute creatures. How much more alive the ocean was when one looked at eye level instead of just the sweeping expanse of sand and water. Like the prairies, she thought. You can only see how alive they really are when you stop looking at the horizons and examine what's at your feet.

She followed Jesse with avid interest. They climbed over the rough black rock that was sharp with small jagged points in many places. Jesse continued his lecture when they reached another pool. 'Now these are starfish.' He pointed to several about the size of his hand attached vertically to the black rock in orange and purple clusters. 'What they do to eat is fold their arms over the intended victim—barnacles in this case—and evert their stomachs into the shell, breaking it up. Digest it on the spot.' He laughed at Stefanie's disgusted expression and gently extracted one for her examination. 'Here—hold it,' he said, thrusting it upon her.

Stefanie took it gingerly. It was surprisingly hard to the touch and as her revulsion died, she looked at it with interest. 'Are these the feet?' she asked, pointing to the many tiny tubes on the underside.

Jesse nodded, his smile warm as he looked at the bright head bent over the starfish. 'They attach themselves to the shell of their intended supper with the feet. They cause a lot of havoc in commercial oyster beds—but no one has come up with a good way to kill them. If they're torn apart and thrown back into the water, they simply regenerate—grow back the missing parts,' he added at Stefanie's puzzled look.

'Interesting,' Stefanie agreed as she put the starfish back in the pond. She sat back on her knees and looked closely at him. 'What else can you show me, professor?' She watched with a pleasure that surprised her as his eyes crinkled at the corners with amusement.

'It shows, does it?' he asked with a rueful grin.

'You mean you really are a teacher?' She wasn't surprised.

'I taught high school biology for a few years,' he admitted. 'And I teach a couple of courses in marine biology at the University in Vancouver.' He grinned.

'Maybe it's just as well I took a year off to write—if it's getting that obvious!'

'To be honest, I'm enjoying it. If only all classrooms were like this,' Stefanie said, gesturing with enthusiasm, 'school would have been fun!'

'You've finished school?'

'Sure have, Mr Stuart.' Stefanie ignored a tiny warning voice and continued with the farce. 'I even managed to get a job in Vancouver before coming over here.' She tried to get the look of pride and pleasure a young person would have at the thought of leaving school and childhood behind.

'Your parents don't mind you moving so far from them?'

Stefanie shrugged. Having gone this far she might as well keep on. 'Not really. They—they'll probably come out soon to make sure I'm okay. But I can take care of myself.' That much was true anyway.

'Sure you can—as long as you stay off rocks when the tide is coming in. And stop opening your door to strange men,' he added with a twinkle in his eyes.

Stefanie flushed, but strangely enough it was because of the sudden memory of his intimate look as she had stood, sleepy and defenceless, in the open doorway.

'Don't worry,' Jesse reassured her, misreading the cause of her embarassment. 'You're forgiven.' He shifted the pack on his back and reached in to extract a camera. 'I'm going to take pictures now—you go and explore. See if you can find anything interesting.' He turned away from her and began adjusting his camera.

Feeling much like a child sent off to play so it wouldn't get in the way, Stefanie scrambled over the rock until she was some distance away. She sat beside a clear pool and stared, not really seeing, into its shallow depth, a frown putting a fine line on her brow.

Jesse Stuart was fast becoming an enigma to her. The first two times she had seen him, he had been cold—mocking her with both his eyes and his words. But since the episode with Pete and the birds yesterday he had become—well, certainly friendly. She had a sudden picture of all her 'uncles' as she grew up in the mining camps, and chuckled. This morning had been very reminiscent of those childhood days when she had been allowed to tag along. It must be the braids, she thought with a smile, examining the end of one auburn plait. Lots of women wore their hair in French braids these days, but they usually pinned them up for a more sophisticated look. Well, she thought with a shrug, maybe it's better like this.

Better? Safer. Jesse Stuart was a virile and sensuous man—she had seen that clearly when he had looked at her dripping wet body in the clinging clothes that first day. She couldn't prevent a shiver from running down her back. If he realised just how much closer in age they really were . . .

Stefanie sat up suddenly and shook her head to clear it of unexpected thoughts. Thoughts of sensuous lips hidden in a tangle of glossy beard, of broad shoulders and lean hips in snug and faded jeans . . . She got up and walked quickly back over the rocks, feeling restless in a way she never had before.

She watched Jesse for a moment. He was lying full length on the rock, carefully holding the camera over the water, focusing on one of the inhabitants. He took a quick series of shots and turned to smile at her. He really has a beautiful smile, she thought, it's so warm and—and gentle.

'That's done,' he said, standing up and brushing sand from his clothes. 'I'm going to drive into Tofino and get this film mailed for processing. It takes a good week or more to get them back, so I like to send them as soon as they're finished. Want to come?' He was bent over the camera rewinding the film.

Stefanie hesitated, not sure whether she should accept the casual invitation. Jesse looked up and smiled. 'C'mon,' he coaxed. 'I'll show you where you can get some fresh seafood. Crabs, shrimp, salmon—and if we're lucky, prawns.'

Stefanie's hesitation fled at the mention of food. Already her mouth was watering at the thought of steaming white crab meat dipped in melted butter, of prawns deep-fried to a golden brown and smothered with lemon sauce. 'There's no way I can resist,' she admitted with a laugh. 'Let's go!'

They took Jesse's truck into town. The highway ran just off the water and they passed several resorts. Jesse explained that the area was left to the local residents— fishermen and loggers—during the winter and early spring, but come May the place overflowed with tourists. Pacific Rim Park campground was always full, as were most of the privately run ones outside the park.

People became a problem when the idea of a national park was to protect an area and keep it as natural as possible, he told her as they drove slowly along the winding road. But on the other hand everyone had a right to enjoy nature and experience it first-hand. The only way around the problem was to educate the public to come, to look and to leave, making sure everything remained as undisturbed as possible.

'And that's where your booklet comes in,' Stefanie finished for him.

'Right,' he grinned. 'You learn fast.'

Stefanie found Tofino delightful. The tiny village was spread out on the edge of an inlet, and had everything one could possibly need. While Jesse checked his mail and made a few purchases at the co-op store, Stefanie walked down to the government wharf and out over the water. She stood watching two young boys fishing off the dock. They had a pile of tubular growths beside them and willingly informed Stefanie that the worms made great bait, laughing at her exaggerated grimace of disgust.

She rested her arms on the railings and felt the sun warm her back. She looked down into the clear water watching shadowy fish swim in and out of the barnacle encrusted pilings. The warm air was a mixture of smells, of salt, fish and tar. She was aware of Jesse coming to stand beside her and for a moment they shared the quiet.

'Come on,' he said finally. 'There's someone I want you to meet.' Without waiting for a response from her, he led the way, taking the incline from the wharf easily with his long stride.

'Hold on!' Stefanie puffed from behind him. 'I'm a prairie girl, remember. I'm used to nice flat streets—not these second cousins to ski slopes!'

Jessie slowed his pace with a laugh and they walked a little farther before turning into a yard at the top of the hill. Stefanie followed him on to the wooden porch of the tiny, brown house, Not knowing what to expect, she stood silently as he knocked on the door and pushed it open without waiting for an answer.

'Aggie?' he called. 'You home?'

'Sure I'm home. Where else?' a voice answered from within.

Jessie pushed the door open wider and went in. Stefanie followed slowly, unsure of herself. They entered a plain but painfully neat living room filled with old-fashioned furniture. An old woman, short, round and brown, beckoned to them from a room at the back of the house. 'Come in, come in,' she invited. She put her hands on Jesse's arms and pulled him down, giving him a resounding kiss on his cheek. 'Eh, Jesse—it's been too many days you don't come.' She turned to Stefanie. 'Who's this?' she asked bluntly, crossing dimpled arms over her ample bosom.

'Stefanie—found her wandering around the beach at my place. Seems to need looking after,' he added with a grin, ignoring Stefanie's indignant expression. 'I thought you could give her a cup of tea while I go talk to Tom.' With a casual wave he left by the back door.

Thanks a lot! Stefanie thought as she watched through the window as he went down the hill to a little dock at the bottom. She turned to smile at Aggie, who was still regarding her closely with a stoical look in her shining black eyes. 'I'm Stefanie Hart,' she said by way of a better introduction. 'And he didn't find me—I'm renting the place next to his.' She hesitated for a moment and then added, 'He—he seems to think I'm much younger than I am.' This woman would not be fooled for an instant.

'Men don't see so good sometimes,' Aggie agreed with a shrug. 'Me, now, I see that you are not such a young girl. But, I think, maybe not yet a woman, eh?'

She gestured towards the large wooden table under the picture window. 'Sit down, sit down. I make tea.' She went to the oil stove in the corner of the room, removed the bubbling kettle and poured water into a big brown tea pot.

Stefanie took a chair that allowed her to look out over the water. For some reason Aggie didn't seem overly concerned that Jesse was mistaken about her right age. Oh well, she dismissed, I guess it's just not that important. She looked out over the water, thinking that it would be a very nice place to live. Even now fishing boats with their trolling poles erect were chugging into the harbour for the night. She smiled her thanks as Aggie placed a mug of steaming dark brew in front of her. She added milk and accepted a ginger snap from the proffered plate. Anxious to break the silence, she asked, 'Have you known Mr—Jesse long?'

'A long time,' Aggie stated in her curious accent, sitting down in the chair opposite Stefanie. 'He come often with my grandson Tom. They fish, swim together all the time when they kids. Still friends.' She nodded towards the little dock where the two men stood. Stefanie saw Jesse throw his head back and laugh at something the other man said.

'Jesse always spend his summers here with his grandpa,' Aggie went on. 'Went to school in Vancouver in winter.'

'Does he live here all the time now?'

'This the first winter he stay. He usually jus' come in summer.' Aggie shook her head. 'For a long time he didn't come even in summer—after he married that Wanda,' she added with a frown.

So there was a wife. The thought was curiously deflating. 'Where is his wife now?' Stefanie knew she was asking a lot of questions about him, but ... It seemed like a perfect opportunity, and Aggie didn't seem to mind.

Aggie shrugged her rounded shoulders. 'That marriage was bad from the start—didn't last. She run off with some man, then they both die in a car crash. A long time ago already.' She got up to refill their cups.

'Jesse, he don't say much about it, but he was not happy for a long, long time. Even now he stays away from women too much. Not good, that—he's too much a man.' She sat back down and looked at Stefanie for a shrewd moment. 'Maybe it's a good thing you look so young, like a girl. He's not worried you might chase him.'

Stefanie grinned at the older woman. 'So what's he going to do when he finds out—start running?'

The woman grinned back at her, a flash of white teeth in her round brown face. 'Maybe by then he don't run so fast, eh?'

But I will, Stefanie thought with a pang that she quickly stilled, and managed to laugh with Aggie. They were still laughing and chattering away with ease when Jesse joined them.

'Now, Aggie, before you pour me a cup of tea, we have to leave. I promised Stefanie some fresh fish, and if we don't go now, we'll be too late.' He held up a hand to stop her protests. 'I promise I'll stop next time I'm in town and drink a whole potful with you.' He reached over and grabbed a cookie from the plate, snapping it in half with his strong white teeth. 'Okay?'

'Okay by me,' Aggie agreed, getting up. 'Bring this one back too, eh?'

They walked back to the truck in silence. Funny, thought Stefanie as she tried to match his long stride, he sure doesn't look like a man who's off women—or did Aggie mean that he had been in the past? She took a quick glance at his strong profile and proudly held head. But, she thought with a smile, I can certainly see women wanting to chase him!

'Has Aggie lived here for long?' she asked as they drove away. 'She seems to have some sort of accent.'

Jesse nodded, keeping an eye on the road as he manoeuvred through the sparse traffic. 'She's a Nootka Indian,' he explained. 'Her people have lived along this coast for countless generations. She married Henri Dupuis when she was just a girl and he taught her to speak French—so English in really her third language, and she learned it fairly late in life.'

'I thought she sounded French some of the time, but I couldn't place it. She's very nice.'

Jesse agreed. 'She's been a good friend to me most of my life. She'll be your friend too—she meant it when she said she'd like you to come back.'

'I'll be sure to do that. Is this the fish place?' she asked as they turned off the road and parked on yet another hill.

'Down there,' said Jesse, pointing to a big warehouse near the water. 'That's the fish packaging plant. The boats have just come in, so we should be in luck. Let's go see what we can get.'

A short time later they were driving back. Stefanie had purchased a pound or so of fresh prawns and one gleaming silver salmon. 'Pete and I are going to eat well tonight,' she said with satisfaction.

'Pete being that piratical black beast of yours, I assume,' remarked Jesse.

'He's not really,' Stefanie protested in defence of her pet. 'He's generally just fat and lazy.'

'From the size of him, I have to believe it!' Jesse laughed.

They made the rest of the drive in relative silence. Stefanie found herself feeling very relaxed with this man, which she still found surprising after the way she had reacted to their first two accidental meetings. But then, she reasoned dryly, since he's decided that I'm just a simple seventeen-year-old in dire need of his tutelage in order to survive his precious ocean, he's been a much nicer person! She could never have been so comfortable with the man she had first thought him to be—even now, the thought of those cold grey eyes raking over her caused a shiver of apprehension to run down her spine.

'Now,' he said as he pulled up her driveway and stopped beside her car, 'are you sure you know how to cook seafood?'

'Sure do, Mr Stuart. We don't live on perogies and potatoes in Winnipeg, you know.'

'Well, I hope you enjoy it,' he said as she opened the door. 'And Stefanie—one more thing. Please stop calling me Mr Stuart! It makes me feel like I'm back in the classroom. Jesse will do just fine.'

Stefanie laughed. 'Okay—Jesse. Thanks very much for today. I enjoyed it.'

'So did I.'

'Don't sound so surprised,' she teased lightly. 'I'm not that bad!'

'No, Stefanie, you're not,' laughed Jesse, and with a thoughtful look on his face, drove away.

The next day was dull and grey, much different from yesterday's sunshine. Stefanie had resigned herself to an afternoon of reading or writing letters to friends. She had just settled down with a pen and good intentions when she heard a knock on the door.

'Mr—Jesse!' she exclaimed with surprise. She hadn't expected to see him again so soon.

'Hello, Stefanie,' he smiled down at her. 'It's your friendly neighbourhood professor looking for students—want to go for a walk?'

'But it's raining,' she protested, looking at the light rain sweeping along the driveway.

'So? If you wait for sunshine out here, you'll never see anything. How about it?'

'Okay,' she agreed without hesitation. He had been good, undemanding company yesterday and a walk along the beach in the rain sounded better the more she thought about it. 'Come in while I get my coat.'

She ran quickly upstairs and pulled on a thick white sweater over the skimpy T-shirt she wore with her jeans. Her boots and coat were in the kitchen, so after a hasty pat to smooth her braided hair, she ran back down, to find Jesse and the cat eyeing each other warily.

'Are you sure this thing is allowed to run loose?' he asked doubtfully. 'It looks like a panther!'

'Looks only,' Stefanie laughed as he gingerly rubbed the cat between the ears. 'He's pure-bred powder-puff— I've seen him run from cats half his size.'

'Half his size is nothing to sneer at!' said Jesse with a hint of admiration. The cat tipped the scale at twenty-five shiny black pounds.

Stefanie pulled on her bright green windbreaker, tucked the ends of her auburn braids under the hood and tied it under her chin.

'Ready?' asked Jesse, getting to his feet.

'Ready.' She grabbed the cat and put him outside as they left.

'Is he coming?'

'I doubt it,' she shrugged. 'He'll probably sit on the stairs looking hurt until I get back. He thinks he should be allowed to hibernate on any day that's more than twenty per cent cloudy!'

The rain wasn't very heavy after all. It was more of a mist that fell to the ground in soft wisps of moisture. It was rather pleasant, Stefanie thought as they walked down to the beach. It was invigorating and not at all cold.

'Are we going anywhere in particular?' she asked, walking quickly to keep up with Jesse's long strides.

'No.' He shook his curly head. 'Just walking.'

'Well, could you just walk, then?' she asked mildly. 'Now I know how my shorter friends used to feel—they were always telling me to slow down!'

Jesse chuckled, his eyes narrow with amusement. 'How's this?' he asked, matching his stride to hers.

'Better,' Stefanie acknowledged with a smile. She resisted an urge to reach out and tuck her hand under his arm. Little girls don't walk arm in arm with the teacher, she told herself with a grin. But, she thought, looking at him from the corner of her eyes, under any other circumstances it wouldn't be a bad idea. She felt a stirring of surprise that the thought had even crossed her mind. Usually she was going out of her way to avoid any sort of physical contact with a man.

For a while she searched for things to say to the tall man beside her, but soon realised it wasn't necessary. The silences between them were comfortable and idle chatter wasn't necessary.

Stefanie bent down suddenly to pick up a small cone-shaped shell. 'What's this?' she asked holding it out on the palm of her hand.

'Limpet,' he answered promptly.

She stuck it on the end of one finger. 'It looks like a hat.'

'Most kids call it a Chinese hat,' he admitted, looking at her with gentle amusement. She didn't look much older than the kids he had in mind, with her hair tucked under her hood. Her cheeks were pink and glowed with the mist that clung to their softness. Her eyes reflected the green of her jacket and sparkled brightly as she smiled at him.

'Is that all you can tell me about them, professor?' she teased.

'Let's see now.' He thought for a moment and then, with a twinkle in his grey eyes, droned in lecture tone, 'A limpet is a marine gastropod mullusc with a low conical shell broadly open beneath, that browses over rocks in the littoral area and adheres tightly when disturbed.'

'No kidding!' Stefanie wrinkled her nose at him.

'No kidding,' he said, his eyes crinkling at the corners. 'Anything else you want to know?'

'I'll be sure to ask,' she said dryly, and slipped the tiny shell into her pocket.

It seemed as though they walked for miles before they turned to go back. Often they were silent, listening to the muffled roar of crashing waves or the high-pitched call of low-flying gulls. Stefanie found herself enjoying his company immensely. She stilled the little voice inside that tried to warn her to end the charade she had started. It was pleasant to be with a man just as a friend. He treated her with an easy warmth, as though he found her somewhat amusing, and it suited her.

If he knew how old I really was . . . Stefanie stopped right there. She didn't need a handsome and obviously virile man making unwanted demands on her. Or did she? The vague restlessness that she had noticed more and more often lately stirred again. Maybe it would take more than a fifteen-hundred-mile move and a change of jobs to still that sense of dissatisfaction—but what? Love and marriage? Stefanie sighed with an unconscious bitter twist to her lips. All she could give was a platonic and sexless love, and what man would want that?

As if sensing her withdrawal, Jesse suggested that they return to his place for a hot drink. Stefanie hesitated for a moment and then accepted. Fine as the mist was, it was beginning to penetrate and she felt uncomfortably damp, and by the time they had tramped through the underbrush to reach his place, the legs of her jeans were soaked.

Jesse opened the back door and ushered her in. 'Give me your jacket,' he said. 'I'll hang it by the fire to dry.' He took it from her and went into the living room. Kneeling on the stone hearth, he stoked up the glowing coals. 'How about a pair of my jeans while those dry?' he suggested when he saw her wet legs.

'Are you kidding?' Stefanie laughed, looking at his long length. 'Even if I tied them under my armpits, I'd still be walking on the knees! These'll be okay,' she added with a smile of thanks. 'They'll dry soon.'

'Suit yourself,' said Jesse, throwing another log on the glowing fire. 'Pull up a chair and make yourself comfortable. I'll go make some coffee.'

Stefanie didn't sit down right away. She wandered around the room, examining it with interest. It was a pleasant room, comfortable as opposed to stylishly decorated. There was a worn leather couch covered with sheepskins and colourful cushions facing the fireplace. Two overstuffed and cosy-looking armchairs stood on each side and on the polished wooden floor in front of the hearth there was a bright braided rug.

She wandered over to the big bay window that faced the ocean. It wasn't as spectacular as the ones in her place, but the view was as nice, and she suspected that when the winter winds blew from the north-west, it probably kept out a lot more of the cold. Right under the window was a big oak table he was obviously using as a desk. Stefanie resisted the urge to glance through the neatly stacked papers beside the typewriter, and wandered around the rest of the room.

The varnished cedar walls were made even more attractive with several well done prints of West Coast

Indian art. 'These are good,' she remarked, turning to Jesse as he came in loaded down with a coffee tray complete with an assortment of cookies.

He nodded as he set the tray down and came to stand beside her. 'Rose did them—she's engaged to Aggie's grandson, Tom. She's been studying fine arts in Victoria,' he added. 'She's finished this year and is coming back to stay. Needless to say, Tom is overjoyed.'

'Aggie said you and Tom have been friends for a long time.'

'Most of our lives. This,' he said, waving a hand around, 'was my grandfather's place. I used to spend my summers—and any other time I could wangle—out here with him. Tom and I were usually together. It was like heaven to be here after being stuck in Vancouver for the school year.'

Stefanie could understand that. The wilderness and freedom the West Coast of Vancouver Island offered would be considered ideal by most young children. She looked at the rugged bearded man beside her and could see that he would fight the restricting bonds of city life.

'Is your grandfather still living?' she asked as they sat down opposite each other in the big chairs flanking the roaring fire.

'No,' said Jesse, handing her a steaming mug of coffee. 'He died a few years ago.' He was silent for a moment. 'He left me this place—he knew I loved it as much as he did. Funny,' he added reflectively, staring into the fire, 'sometimes I think he's still here.'

'He probably is,' said Stefanie. 'If he loved it that much.'

Jesse looked across at her with just a hint of seriousness in his smiling eyes. 'Do you really think so?'

'Why not?' she shrugged, and reached for a cookie. 'If I have a choice—after—I'd hang around the place I loved best.'

'And where would that be?'

Stefanie frowned, thinking of all the temporary places she had lived with her father. 'I don't really know,' she had to admit. 'We moved around so much.'

'What does your father do?'

'He was—is,' she corrected hastily, 'a mining engineer. We lived in Northern Manitoba—in the bush mainly.'

'And that's why the isolation here doesn't bother you,' Jesse said, nodding. 'I wondered about that—not many girls your age would take kindly to being so alone.'

'It doesn't bother me a bit,' Stefanie said truthfully. Indeed, it had never even occurred to her—she had been alone for so long.

'Weren't there any boy-friends in Winnipeg anxious to come and keep you company?' Jesse asked lazily. He was sitting back in his chair regarding her with idle curiosity.

'Oh, sure. Lots and lots,' said Stefanie, her eyes gleaming with hidden laughter. 'Let's see,' she went on, counting on her fingers, 'there was Bob and Raymond and Phil and . . .'

'Okay, okay, I get the picture,' Jesse laughed, raising his hands in surrender. 'You like to play the field.'

'Don't you?' Stefanie's innocent question belied a growing curiosity.

'It's always been my best position,' he drawled, 'but I don't mind an occasional stint at home plate.'

She was puzzled for a moment and then she remembered the vernacular. She felt a surprising warmth stain her cheeks and hurriedly picked up a cookie, nibbling quickly in an attempt to hide her confusion.

Jesse, as if taking pity on her embarrassment, changed the subject, barely concealing his humour. He carried the conversation easily. He was both amusing and informative as he told Stephanie some of the local history of the west coast of the Island. She listened with interest as she heard for the first time how Captain James Cook discovered the area late in the eighteenth century, and learned that Spain and England had both laid claim to the territory, Britain winning possession in the end. He talked comfortably, discussing rather than lecturing, using his well shaped hands for quiet emphasis. His intelligence was obvious, and Stefanie felt that if he wrote half as descriptively as he spoke, he must be very successful.

She didn't realise how late it was getting until Jesse turned on the lamp beside him. After a surprised glance at the burl clock above the fireplace, she started to tell him it was time she was leaving, but the shrill ring of the telephone interrupted her.

Jesse reached out a lazy hand and picked up the receiver. 'Hello? Louisa! I'm glad you called—hang on a sec, will you?' He put his hand over the mouthpiece and turned to Stefanie as she hastily slipped into her jacket.

'I was just going,' she said brightly. 'Thanks for everything.'

''Bye, Stefanie,' he said with a slow smile. 'See you around.' With a casual wave he turned his attention back to the caller.

Louisa—who is she? Stefanie wondered as she went through the kitchen to the door. It was obvious from the warmth she could hear in the rumble of his deep voice that her call was welcome. She hesitated with her hand on the door knob, tempted for an instant to eavesdrop, but knowing that she shouldn't linger any longer, she slipped quietly out through the door.

Somehow the phone call had caused the visit to end on an unsatisfactory note. Why? Stefanie shrugged as she trudged down the path between the two houses. All she knew was that she had enjoyed Jesse's company to a surprising extent. After the first two meetings she had been sure his presence would be a blight on her well earned holiday, but now she found herself hoping it wouldn't be long before he came around to collect her for another tour. He was good company—amusing, intelligent—and safe.

I think I've been adopted, she thought dryly as she carefully skirted the dripping trees. A twinge of guilt pricked at her conscience as she thought of how she was allowing a friendship to grow on dishonesty. With a sense of disquiet she began to realise that she was heading straight for trouble. How was Jesse going to react when he found out he had been duped? Stefanie had no doubt that for all his apparent good nature, he wouldn't take kindly to being played the fool. And that was exactly what she was doing.

With a sigh of indecision she crossed the driveway to her back door. She knew she should be honest with him. At first it hadn't made any difference, but in the light of their growing amity she should tell him the truth about her age. But if he knew . . .

And why, she asked herself mockingly, are you so sure he would treat you any differently? But there would be a difference. She knew she hadn't mistaken the vibrant sensuality hovering beneath his gentle façade. She shivered delicately as she remembered again how his eyes had lingered on her breasts, sharply moulded by the translucency of her wet T-shirt. It was a look she did not want to see on any man's face.

Her reverie was cut short by a sharp miaow of indignation. With a laugh that dispelled her doubts, Stefanie bent down to pet her damp cat.

'Why didn't you get out of the rain, you silly puss?' She went into the house, followed closely by the cat, who sat beside his empty dish, staring at her accusingly until she took pity on him and gave him a generous serving of his favourite food.

Her own supper that night was simple and scrumptious. She cleaned yesterday's prawns, boiled them in salted water and dipped them in lemon butter, washing them down with cool white wine. After cleaning up she felt a surge of inexplicable restlessness, a feeling that was becoming all to familiar.

Even a hot bath failed to have its usual soothing effect. What's wrong with me? she asked herself as she stepped out of the tub. A puzzled frown marred her smooth brow as she towelled herself dry. The feeling wasn't anything as simple as boredom. It went deeper than that, an intensification of the same feeling she had felt before leaving Winnipeg. She felt restless, dissatisfied and—lonely? In an effort to cheer herself up, she ignored the comfort of her velour robe and chose instead a caftan of thin cream-coloured silk shot through with fine gold thread. A slender cord pulled through slits in the sides and tied in front, allowing the back to flow freely while pulling the bodice firmly over her breasts. She unbraided her hair and brushed it into a copper cloud that danced softly over her shoulders and down her back.

She put down the brush and stared at her reflection. Picking up her glass, she took a sip of wine, moodily wondering about herself. She was alone, just as she had chosen to be, and at this moment it was very unsatisfying. Scowling at herself, she got up slowly and wandered down into the kitchen to pour the last of the wine into her glass.

Without bothering with the lights, she crumbled paper on to the grate of the fireplace and piled on cedar kindling. As she touched a match to the paper, cherry flames began to crackle, pushing some of the gloom into the background. Fire roaring, Stefanie turned to her stereo. It was an expensive piece of electronic equipment, a real indulgence. Her music collection ranged from the traditional classics to the latest rock, with everything from country to jazz in between. Music was a joy to her, at times a passion, a medium through which she could express the pent-up emotions denied release in other ways.

She dropped a Johann Strauss album on to the turntable and turned up the volume until the melodious strains of dreamy waltzes filled the air. Too restless to just sit and listen, she roamed around the room, drink in hand, her body beginning to sway in time to the music, aching to dance. Following the mesmeric commands of the music, Stefanie set down the glass, and with a deep curtsey, entered a glittering ballroom in bygone Vienna. She laughed up into the eyes of the man who swept her on to the dance floor, and danced, enraptured and oblivious to all.

She didn't hear the knock, nor notice the back door open. She didn't see the man standing just beyond the louvred doors in the kitchen watching silently as she turned and swirled over the polished floor in the arms of an invisible lover.

His hesitation was obvious. By rights, he knew, he should go quietly and leave her to her fantasy, but the pull of her enchantment was strong. He was drawn to the glimmer of gossamer light she made in the dimness of the room as the firelight flickered on the gold threads of her robe. As she moved the thin silk moulded to the soft roundness of her limbs, and his eyes narrowed as he watched the exquisiteness of her unconscious grace. He knew he must leave and turned as though to go, but instead he moved closer until he stood before her.

Her start of surprise was obvious as she stopped off balance. Jesse's hands reached out to cup her shoulders in a steadying clasp. Still under the spell of the swelling music, Stefanie stood still in his hold, looking up at him, her eyes wide and luminous in the pearly paleness of her face. When she made as though to speak, he placed a gentle finger over her lips and with a bemused smile began to waltz with her.

Feeling, not thinking, Stefanie was caught in a sensuous web. With a will of its own her body responded to the commands of his rugged grace. Her fingers splayed over the rippling muscles of his back, and it was with an effort that he restrained himself from pulling her closer.

Stefanie danced as she never had before. Never had she felt so aware of a man and she fairly floated on the currents that flowed between them. With a final crescendo the music began to fade, and they slowed almost reluctantly and finally stopped.

Stefanie could only stare at Jesse, conscious of the heat of his hands on her hips and back. Her lips were softly parted and her eyes dazed and somewhat incredulous at the sensations coursing through her. Her rapid heart beat and the unsteadiness of her legs were caused by more than the exertion of the dance. Jesse's eyes were drawn from her face to linger on the fluttering pulse in her smooth white throat. Under his gaze she felt her breasts grow full and taut as they pushed against the thin silk of her robe. Without will, she swayed towards him.

All too aware of her youth and sensing the innocence

behind the desire in her eyes, Jesse kept control, knowing he should have gone. Slowly he raised her hand to his lips and pressed a lingering kiss on the soft skin of her inner wrist. And then, with a light mocking smile, he left.

Stefanie stood rooted to the spot, unconsciously rubbing her wrist over her tremulous lips, confused by the emotions tumbling through her. Something had stirred in her during that dance, something she had never felt before; something she had despaired of ever feeling. Suddenly a light laugh of pure joy bubbled from her lips and she twirled around to run quickly upstairs. The feeling was too fragile, too precious to analyse. Hugging it to her, she slipped into bed and fell asleep, a soft smile on her lips.

CHAPTER FOUR

IN spite of the ease with which she fell asleep, Stefanie spent a restless night. She relived the dance many times in her dreams, each time seeing desire, not restraint, in the piercing grey eyes. And this time when she swayed towards Jesse, he clutched her tight against his hard body and his lips touched not her wrist but her mouth, enveloping her in fire.

With a stifled moan she sat up in bed. She pushed the heavy fall of hair back from her face and shook her head to clear the residue of subconscious desire. All this from one dance! she thought, swinging her legs from the tangle of bedclothes. She went to shower, still wondering at the effect this virtual stranger had on her.

How much had she given away to him last night? She moved uneasily under the spray of hot water. She had been too taken by surprise both by his sudden appearance and the intensity of the feelings stirred by sharing that perfect dance with him to effectively mask her response.

She frowned as she stepped out of the shower and towelled herself dry. That the evening had ended as it did was due entirely to Jesse's control. If he had known just how much closer in age they actually were . . .

Stefanie felt a tiny shudder run through her at the thought of the response his lips would have demanded, of the pliancy he would have expected as he crushed her body against his. For a second she wished it had been that way.

Sure, and then what? Her smile was harsh. Did she really want him to see what would follow, to have him watch the nauseating fear that would wash over her in wave after humiliating wave? Twice before a man had kissed her with passion, and both times the results had been disastrous. She would not allow it to happen

57

again. She finished dressing with hands that shook and went downstairs.

There wasn't much point in telling Jesse the truth about her age, Stefanie realised with a bitter twist to her lips. The reality was that emotionally and sexually she wasn't much more than the child he took her for. She was no more capable of a normal response to a man's passion than she was of flying.

Damn Frank Dawson! Stefanie stood up, her eyes glittering with angry tears. Was she never to be free of his attack? It had effectively destroyed her ability to be a normal loving woman. Reaching for her jacket, she walked blindly from the house. Why had no one ever thought of the consequences? Everyone who knew about the attack had been so relieved that actual rape had been prevented that they hadn't even considered the possibility of emotional damage.

Guilt—that was what it was. No one but Stefanie knew how she had responded to Dawson's first tentative kisses. She had been surprised when he had leaned over to kiss her lightly on the mouth. This first kiss had intrigued her and she had responded with innocent pleasure. It was only when the kisses had become insistent and he thrust a rough hand under her shirt to fondle her tender breasts that she had started to panic and begged him to stop.

He had turned ugly then. He cursed her, calling her a tease, a slut and many other names too horrible to remember. He struck her ruthlessly across the face, not once but several times, tearing at her clothes with brutal lust.

Stefanie shuddered violently at the vivid memory. She sat down on a beached log, rubbing a trembling hand across her eyes in a vain attempt to dry the tears that flowed as she remembered. For the first time since the horrifying assault she really remembered. If ever there had been a time in her young life when she had needed a mother that was it, but there had been no woman to turn to. Instead, she had been forced into what seemed like exile, away from the father she cherished. Feeling forsaken and unbearably guilty, she had forced the real memory of that day deep inside, burying it along with all the passions and desires a developing woman should have felt.

And suddenly, because a man she scarcely knew had danced with her, it was all beginning to surface, tearing painfully at the defences that had become deeply rooted over the years. Helpless against the onslaught of bitter memory. Stefanie rose again and walked the beach aimlessly, seeking release from the pain.

It was hours later when she returned. She was exhausted but more at peace with herself. Reliving those most painful of memories had absolved her of misplaced guilt, but she knew that until she could overcome the fear of intimate contact with a man, she wasn't free of Dawson's contamination. Tony, she had come to realise, was merely incidental—a shallow, self-satisfying man who, in restrospect, hadn't made much difference in her life.

Stefanie climbed wearily into bed. It was early, but she was tired—tired of thinking, tired of memories, just plain tired. I need a man, she thought with grim humour as she slipped between the sheets. Unbidden, she saw Jesse's strong face before her, saw his grey eyes that could be so soft and gentle when he smiled at her. She remembered again the vibrant touch of his lips against her wrist at the end of that magical dance.

So what do I do? she asked herself with a bitter smile. Tell him all the sordid details and beg him to be gentle? He'd pat me on the head and tell me to be a good girl and go home to Daddy!

The day had been emotionally painful and exhausting. Stefanie fell asleep quickly, scarcely conscious of the tears dampening the pillow beneath her cheek.

She lay in bed for a long time the next morning, very still and quiet. She thought long and hard about what she had gone through yesterday and realised that forcing herself to relive those horrific memories was probably the start of the real healing process. When she finally did get up, she felt calm an almost trancelike, drained of all emotion.

She went through the motions of the day feeling little.

She lay on the cushions in front of a roaring blaze listening to music, glad there were no visitors to see her in such a vulnerable state. She was vaguely aware of a detached feeling, almost as if she was elsewhere, watching her body in languid pose on the floor in front of the hearth. Finally she managed to drag herself into the kitchen to choke down a bowl of soup, and then it was back to bed and instant oblivion.

It was exactly what she needed. She awoke the next day full of vigour and feeling an underlying excitement. She knew that the past was really behind her now, and while her emotional growth might have been slightly stunted over the years, she was going to come out ahead.

She took a leisurely shower and shampooed her hair. She sat in front of the mirror blow-drying her hair until it settled like a silken cape over her bare shoulders. With deft fingers she rolled it into a simple knot at the base of her neck, allowing wispy strands to curl softly around her face. She hesitated, then almost defiantly applied eye-shadow, mascara and a trace of blusher along her cheekbones.

Finally she dressed and stood in front of the mirror, smiling with satisfaction. She had tucked an ivory camisole into soft khaki slacks and added a matching bush jacket and square-cut tan leather boots. The transformation from girl to woman was amazing.

'No grubby little girl today, Pete,' she informed the cat, curled up and oblivious to all on the wide bed. 'I'm going to town!'

Still bouyant after a quick breakfast, Stefanie hopped into her car and drove into Tofino. She went slowly, savouring the sunshine that streaked through the trees and rebounded with a diamond dazzle from the calm blue water. She stopped at the little co-op store for a few groceries, and then, hungry for companionship, went over to Aggie's, parking on the hill in front of the little brown house. She knocked tentatively on the door, hoping Aggie wouldn't mind her dropping in. She needn't have worried.

The old woman answered the door, wiping her hands

on her voluminous apron. 'Eh, Stefanie—come in, come in.' She beamed her welcome and held the door open wide. 'Jesse, he say you might come by.'

'Thanks, Aggie,' Stefanie smiled as she went in. 'I'm glad you don't mind me dropping in like this—I really felt like company today.' She followed the woman into the kitchen.

'You want tea?' asked Aggie, pushing the simmering kettle on the back of the oil stove closer to the heat.

'Sure,' Stefanie smiled as she sat down at the table. 'But I came by to ask you out for lunch. Know any good places?'

'One place makes good fish 'n chips,' Aggie said promptly. Apparently the invitation was welcome. 'Fresh fish, real potatoes—not frozen. Sound okay?' She looked expectantly at Stefanie.

'Sounds good to me,' Stefanie laughed. 'It's early yet—how about we go in half an hour?'

Aggie nodded, placing cups, milk and sugar on the table. 'Give us time for tea,' she said, pouring the strong liquid. 'Sugar?'

Stefanie shook her head and watched in amazement as Aggie stirred in three heaped spoonfuls to her own cup.

'Jesse's gone,' Aggie stated, clinking her spoon against the rim of her cup.

Stefanie started. Gone? For good? 'Where?' she managed and took a calming sip of tea.

'Vancouver for a few days.' Aggie told her. 'He don't say much to me. Tom says he's gone to see Louisa—Wanda's sister,' she added by way of explanation. Aggie's black eyes darkened and she scowled. 'Her, I don't like. I tell Jesse, stay away from her, she's like her sister too much.' Suddenly she flashed her wide smile. 'Maybe that's why he don't tell me he's going, eh?'

'Are—are they serious?' Stefanie had to ask. She tried to sound offhand and casual, but failed miserably, remembering how welcome her call had been the other day.

Aggie's bright eyes studied her for a moment, then she gave an eloquent shrug. 'Me, I don't know. They

know each other for a long, long time and she's very
. . .' Her dimpled hands drew an exaggerated picture of
a woman's curves in the air.

Stefanie had to chuckle. 'A regular centre-fold, huh?'

Aggie nodded. 'Tom, he says she's all the time after
Jesse when he's in Vancouver. Come for dinner, come
for party.' She shrugged. 'Who's to know what else?'

Remembering the undoubted sensuality of the man,
Stefanie could well imagine what else, and it was
disheartening. In light of what she had learned about
herself in the last couple of days, she was cautiously
beginning to think that she might be normal. To learn
now that there was a woman—his dead wife's sister
yet—in the life of the man who had so effortlessly
stirred her into awareness, was threatening her new-
found hopes. She took a quick swallow of tea and
changed the subject. She didn't want to hear any more.
'I'm getting hungry,' she said with a quick smile. 'Want
to leave soon?'

'Jus' let me get cleaned up,' said Aggie as she drained
her cup. 'How about you go down to the dock, tell Tom
we're leaving?'

'Okay.' Stefanie rose, placed the cups in the big
porcelain sink and slipped out of the back door. She
stood on the small porch for a moment, looking down
the hill to the water's edge. The dock was little more
than planks and posts extending out far enough to keep
the fishing boat afloat at low tide. She could see
someone, Tom, she assumed, standing over the boat's
engine. Quickly she descended the stairs and followed
the well worn path down the hill.

'Tom?' she called tentatively as she walked out over
the water, and he answered with a casual wave. 'Hi,
Tom. I'm Stefanie,' she said easily. 'Your gr . . .'

'Stefanie?' he interrupted. 'You're the little redhead
staying next to Jess?' He stared at her.

'That's me!' Stefanie stood smiling at his incredulous
look, tall and slim with her hands jammed casually into
her pockets and the sun striking a thousand fiery sparks
from her hair.

Tom straightened up still staring at her as he wiped

his hands clean on a rag. He was slightly shorter than she was with straight black hair and a muscular build. He shook his head in disbelief. 'I've never known Jess to be wrong about much, but . . .'

'I gather he wasn't exactly complimentary,' Stefanie said, laughing as an embarrassed Tom tried to explain his friend's remarks. 'It's okay, Tom—really! Somehow Jesse got the impression that I was just a kid and I—er—I haven't set him straight. I guess I should have,' she ended, beginning to feel very guilty.

'Oh, I don't know,' Tom drawled with a grin, showing square white teeth in his brown face. 'I sort of like the idea of ol' Jess being wrong about something for once. Besides, he's played more than one trick on people himself—do him good to be on the receiving end!'

In spite of the fact that Tom seemed to be enjoying the idea, Stefanie remained doubtful. 'I don't know, Tom. I mean, the longer this goes on, the harder it'll be to straighten out.' She sighed. 'I wish it hadn't gone his far!'

Tom gave her a shrewd look reminiscent of his grandmother. 'So tell him,' he said bluntly.

'Will he be very angry?' Tom had been his friend long enough to know, and suddenly Jesse's reaction to her deception had become important.

He shrugged. 'He'll probably go all cold for a while,' he said, confirming her worst fears. He let his eyes travel slowly over her in appreciation. 'But,' he added with a wicked grin, 'he'd be crazy if he didn't like it better!'

Stefanie had to laugh. 'Thanks, Tom!' His obvious admiration boosted her sagging confidence. She glanced up at the house and saw Aggie waving. 'I came down to tell you I'm taking Aggie out for lunch. We shouldn't be late getting back.'

Tom nodded with approval. 'She'll like that. Doesn't always want to go out any more—it'll make nice change for her. Oh—and Stefanie,' he added as she turned to go, 'Rose—my fiancée—will be back from university next week and we'll be having an engagement party.'

He grinned. 'I think Rose is going to like you—consider yourself invited!'

Stefanie smiled with pleasure. 'Thanks, Tom—I'll be glad to go. Just let me know when it is,' she said, and waved goodbye as she went to get Aggie.

Lunch with Aggie was a delight. She might have been lacking in formal education, but she was rich in observations and natural philosophy, recounting stories with a subtle wit to which Stefanie responded with genuine pleasure.

The food was good too. Fresh cod and been deep-fried in a crisp tasty batter and was served with thick golden wedges of potato. Stefanie ate heartily, appetite restored after yesterday's depression.

'I needed that,' she sighed, finally pushing her plate aside. 'I didn't eat much yesterday.'

'Sick?' asked Aggie.

'No, not really,' Stefanie answered. 'Just—down in the dumps, I guess.'

'You got a problem, or just one of those days?'

'Well——' Stefanie hesitated. Was there any need to share what she had come to realise? 'There was a problem,' she admitted, 'but I think it'll be okay now.' I hope, she added fervently to herself.

Aggie nodded, finishing her tea. 'You ever need to talk, I listen,' she assured her.

Stefanie smiled her thanks. 'I just might take you up on that some day,' she promised as she picked up the bill and prepared to pay. 'Are you in a hurry to get back, Aggie? It's such a beautiful day, I thought we might go for a walk on the beach.'

'Sounds okay to me,' Aggie nodded in agreement.

They walked along the water's edge, silent with the comfortable companionship that can spring up between two people regardless of age or circumstance. Stefanie knew she had found a kindred spirit in Aggie, and felt as though she had been a friend for years instead of days.

'Let's sit down,' Aggie pointed her chin towards a natural bench of beached logs. 'My legs, they don't want to walk so far no more.'

'How old are you, Aggie?' Stefanie asked curiously as they sat down, arranging themselves comfortably on the logs.

'Eighty-six, June,' Aggie told her, folding her hands over her ample stomach. They were pleasantly full from their meal, feeling drowsy as the rays of the strengthening sun warmed their backs.

'Then I guess you remember some of the old days.'

Aggie nodded. 'But even in my time there were many changes. Most of the real old times I know from my grandmother. She tell me many many stories about the time when all this belong to the Nootka people.' She waved a hand in the air. 'The cedar trees gave us lodges, clothing, totem poles. But we were of the ocean. From it we took salmon and seals and the whale.'

'Whales? You mean your people hunted whales?' Stefanie looked over the cold expanse of ocean and tried to imagine it.

'When my father was a boy,' Aggie began, 'he and other children watched from the high rocks. When they see the spray from the whale, they signal to the men. Two canoes go out after it. My grandfather, a great chief, stood ready with his harpoon to make the first hit. Each time the whale came up to breathe, the men struck. Finally he would die and be brought to shore. Everyone was very happy. The whale, he make enough oil and meat for many days in winter, and there was much feasting.'

It became a poignant memory for Stefanie, lost in the spell of Aggie's simple tale. She could see the warriors clad in woven cedar-bark capes following their chief on to the open ocean in frail cedar canoes to hunt the giant whales.

They had lived a higher than subsistence life. The ocean and the forest provided a bounty that left time for the people to develop a special and unique art form. Headdresses, ceremonial masks, canoe prows— even the posts and beams of the lodges became works of art, ornately carved and often in laid with shell. Magnificent totem poles were carved from the giant cedar trees, the figures often representing the history of a family from the beginning when Raven created Earth and its people.

What Aggie could tell in her simple but eloquent way was of a way of life gone from its people. Aggie and others like her were the last real links between a strong culture that was, and a culture in the process of a vast and often painful change.

Aggie's sudden sigh brought Stefanie back to the present. 'My family,' she said, 'they lived much like the old. But already there were many changes. So many died from the white man's sickness. Our village was very poor, not so many people left.' Stefanie could hear many past sorrows in her voice.

'I was young, fifteen, when Henri came. He was a good man, very kind. I was happy to go with him.' She smiled at Stefanie. 'We had a good life, make lots of babies. All those babies, they grow up, make more babies.' She gave a philosophical shrug. 'They do all right. Now, enough talk from me.' She gave Stefanie's arm a hearty pat. 'I get too stiff to move, we sit here much longer. Time to go, eh?'

They got up and walked slowly along the water in the direction they had come. 'You going to look like this for Jesse when he came home?' Aggie asked suddenly, commenting on Stefanie's more mature appearance for the first time.

Stefanie sighed a bit and gave a tiny shrug. 'I guess I should tell him,' she said, 'but how do I go about it? I mean—do I break it to him gently, or just spring it on him?' She smiled wryly. 'Either way, he's not going to be too happy about being misled, is he?'

But I want him to know, she thought with a tinge of despair at the predicament she had placed herself in. I want him to know I'm a woman and not a little girl. She remembered dancing with him, how he had lifted her from the bounds of reality straight into fantasy. She could see his strong face, his grey eyes—and most of all, his lithe body moving so sensuously with her, his back muscles rippling under her hand. His . . . Stefanie gave herself a mental shake. This is getting ridiculous! she told herself. Here I am getting all weak in the knees about a man who seems quite happy to think of me as one of his high school biology students? Firmly she thrust the memory from her.

Aggie had been quiet for a moment, thinking. 'I got an idea,' she said suddenly. 'My Tom and his Rosie are getting married soon. There'll be a big party, next week maybe. Jesse'll be there—you come too.' She gave a sly smile, nudging Stefanie with her elbow. 'Then you show him, eh?'

'You know,' said Stefanie thoughtfully, 'that's a good idea. Yes,' she added with a wide smile, 'I think that just might be the best way.' And best of all, the postponement would give her the breathing space she needed to adjust to the growth of new emotions.

CHAPTER FIVE

'ANYBODY home?'

Jesse! Stefanie straightened up from the laundry she was sorting in the tiny utility room off the kitchen. Her stomach jumped nervously at the sound of his voice and her face flushed as her heart stepped up its rhythm. Unconsciously her hands went up to smooth back wisps of hair that had escaped from her ponytail, and she quickly tucked her T-shirt into faded jeans. Taking a deep breath, she went into the kitchen.

Jesse was leaning in the open doorway watching her as she padded barefoot towards him. 'Hi, little girl,' he said with his lopsided grin. 'I see you've managed to stay in one piece while I was gone—which is surprising, considering your penchant for unlocked doors!'

'Hi, Jesse,' she said brightly finding it all too easy to slip back into the role he had given her. 'Aggie said you were in Vancouver. Did you have a good trip?'

'Let's just say it was—successful,' he drawled, and Stefanie, remembering all Aggie had said about Louisa, felt a flush stain her cheeks. She fervently hoped that wasn't the success he meant.

She turned quickly to hide her face from his astute eyes. 'Want some coffee?' she asked diffidently.

'Actually, I'm off to one of the beaches today,' he said shutting the door behind him as he came into the kitchen. 'Want to come?'

Stefanie hesitated. She glanced through the door of the utility room to the pile of laundry waiting for her, then outside at the bright sunshine and blue sky, and then back to Jesse's face. 'Give me five minutes,' she said, going towards the stairs. 'Help yourself to coffee.'

She climbed the stairs slowly, feeling somewhat disappointed that his attitude towards her hadn't changed. She was still 'little girl' in his eyes. She sighed as she slipped into cream-coloured cords and a warm moss green sweater. It was ridiculous to suppose that Jesse would have found the dance they had shared anything other than an amusing interlude. Had he, in fact, laughingly shared the experience with Louisa as they lingered over a romantic dinner?

Stefanie grimaced as she removed her ponytail and brushed her hair into a soft knot. There was no rational reason for the stirrings of jealousy she felt at the thought of him with Louisa, but that didn't stop unwelcome and disturbing pictures from forming in her mind. She jumped up, shaking her head. She would go downstairs and enjoy his company on whatever level he wanted to give it. If friendship was all they could share, then so be it. She wasn't going to try to change things, not at this point. Pasting a bright smile on her face, she returned to the kitchen.

'You look very pretty,' Jesse remarked with approval as she sat on a chair to pull on her boots.

'Why, thank you, sir,' Stefanie dimpled, looking straight at him for the first time since he had walked in. And you, she thought, bending back down to tie a lace, are looking devastatingly handsome! His creamy thick wool sweater set off his dark beard beautifully—and what the tight faded jeans did for his lean hips, she couldn't think about and remain rational.

'There, I'm ready,' she said, standing up quickly. 'Will we be gone long?'

He shrugged. 'A couple of hours. Why?'

'Well, I haven't eaten much today,' she explained, opening the door to the fridge, 'and I'm going to be very hungry, very soon. How about you?'

'Got any apple pie?' he asked hopefully.

'No,' she answered, her voice muffled by the fridge, 'but there's fresh baked bread, cheese and—let's see—some corned beef, pickles . . .' She pulled out the food and set it on the counter.

'Okay, okay,' he laughed. 'Let's have a picnic.'

'Great idea, Jesse,' Stefanie agreed. She began to cut and butter the bread. 'Oh, Jesse—could you go get that cat from the bed? I don't like to leave him in when I go out. Unlikely as it seems, he just might get frisky one of these days and climb up those drapes in the living room—and I'd never get enough for his hide to pay for them!'

Jesse obliged and returned quickly, holding a none too happy cat, legs dangling in mid-air. 'Do I get to throw him, or will he go peacefully?'

'Don't sound so hopeful,' Stefanie laughed. 'A gentle boost will do nicely.'

They drove off in Jesse's truck, a comfortable silence between them. It feels so right to be with him, Stefanie thought. Sometimes it feels as if I've known him for ever—but I really don't know him at all. She turned to look out the side window, catching glimpses of sun-sparkled ocean through the trees. I want to know him, she thought wistfully. I want to know all about him. She turned her head until she could look at him, her eyes wide and vulnerable, and sighed so softly it escaped his attention. But most of all, she thought, I want him to know I'm not a little girl—I want him to know I'm a woman. Now isn't it just too bad, she mocked herself, that I'm just too much of a coward to come right out and tell him?

She was glad when they turned off the highway and parked on a gravel lot beneath towering trees. There was too much she wanted to tell him, and her thoughts were in such a turmoil she was afraid she would blurt the truth out in the worst possible way. Perhaps Aggie's idea was best—just show him. And preferably in a room full of people, she thought dryly, and climbed out of the truck.

A path led to the beach through a thick and tangled forest of green. Ferns grew high and salal crammed itself into every open space. Cedar and hemlock trees grew tall, but all along the path were moss-covered stumps and roots that spoke of even greater giants, logged long ago. It was when she was under this canopy of green that she could, with a sense of awe, truly understand that this was a rain forest. It was almost a relief when they stepped out into the light and bright air of the shoreline.

'This is the nudist beach in the summer,' Jesse told

her as they walked towards a craggy black rock that sloped from the trees and jutted out over the sand to the water.

'Come here often?' Stefanie asked wickedly.

Jesse laughed. 'I've never felt the urge to expose myself publicly.'

'But you do tan in the nude?' she persisted in spite of herself. She could just see that long lean body stretched out in a pool of golden sunshine . . .

'Nosey little girl, aren't you?' he grinned, evading the question, which was as good as an answer as far as she was concerned.

'So do I,' she admitted. 'This beach could be interesting.' She looked around with exaggerated interest, knowing that, like him, she wasn't inclined to strip down on a public beach.

'Like I said—precocious,' he murmured. 'Doesn't your father object?'

'Oh, what Daddy doesn't know won't hurt him,' she said airily. 'I can't tell him everything, can I?' She tilted her head towards him and smiled secretively.

'Brat,' he said mildly.

Stefanie groaned inwardly, disgusted with herself. Instead of trying to ease out of the mess she had got herself into, she was steadily digging herself in deeper. Suddenly she sprinted off. 'Race you to the rock!' she called over her shoulder to a startled Jesse, and was halfway up its steep side before he caught up with her.

'You cheated,' he growled, coming up beside her. 'For that you get to carry this lunch of yours the rest of the way!'

'How about I carry it back?' she asked with a grin.

'When it's empty? Forget it.' He handed her the knapsack.

There was a cave in the vee-shaped cove on the other side of the rock, its shallow depth approachable at low tide. In the rocky niches and recesses of the little cavern, logs and blocks of wood had been wedged in tight by the persistent power of the ocean.

It was the crevice in the rock bounding the far side of the cove that impressed her the most. What had started aeons ago as a crack had eroded until the huge rock was split neatly in two. Cautiously, Stefanie followed Jesse into the opening. She shivered as the damp narrow walls closed around her, and hunched her shoulders to prevent them from rubbing against the dank stone.

They stopped in the middle of the fissure and Jesse pointed to the tidemark high above their heads. It was an eerie feeling. There was sand at their feet and sky above them, but it was a place where the sun never shone. Where, in a few hours the ocean would roll in with all its immense power, gnawing again and again at the black rock until the crack became a chasm.

'I don't like this place,' Stefanie shuddered.

'It's not my favourite place either,' Jesse admitted, 'but at least you don't have to walk sideways!'

It was a relief to emerge into the sun-bright cove. 'I'm going to take pictures now,' Jesse told her. He took his camera out of its case and began to make adjustments.

'Is that a hint to go and play?' Stefanie couldn't help smiling.

'Yes,' he said absently, already focussing the lens. 'Be a good girl and get lunch ready, will you?'

'Yes, sir!' Stefanie made a face at his unsuspecting back and hoisted the knapsack on to her shoulders, leaving him in peace.

They sat on the soft sand behind logs that had been piled into a windbreak. Out of the bite of the wind which was stronger today, the sun was quite warm. Stefanie had spread a blanket and piled food in the middle. There were thick slices of brown bread spread with butter, thinly sliced corned beef, cheese, pickles and a half bottle of white wine. It was a plain but hearty meal, most welcome after a morning in the salty air.

'So—you did go see Aggie while I was gone?' Jesse reached lazily for a piece of cheese.

'Yep,' said Stefanie, sitting cross-legged on the blanket licking pickle brine from her fingers. 'We went out to lunch and a walk on the beach.' She wiped her hands on her jeans and looked at Jesse sincerely. 'She's a fascinating woman, Jesse. We got to talking and she told me about her family—her grandfather leading whale hunts and things like that. Someone should write it down before it's lost.'

'Someone is,' he told her.

'Who?'

'Me.'

'You? I thought you were working on a government booklet.'

'That's just a cash sideline,' he said, dismissing it with a wave. 'I've been working with Aggie for about six months now—we're almost done. In fact,' he continued, 'that was one of the reasons I went to Vancouver this week. I got a publisher interested in the rough draft. Looks like we're in business!'

'That's great!' Stefanie smiled openly at him. 'That definitely calls for a toast.' She raised her glass and intoned. 'May you always be published!' and swallowed the rest of her wine.

'A very appropriate toast for an aspiring author,' he said dryly, taking a more cautious sip of his wine, and with a slight frown asked, 'Do you always drink so much?'

Stefanie looked at him with surprise. She had barely had half a glass. 'What do you mean?'

'Well, this wine today—and when I dropped in the other night when you were—er—dancing, I would say you'd had plenty by then.' His frown had deepened.

Stefanie winced at his offhand remark about the dance they had shared, which to her had been a magical moment suspended in time. Clinging to pride, she managed a light laugh and continued with the role that was becoming far to easy to play. 'Really, Jesse, don't be so fuddy-duddy! You sound just like Daddy,' she said, imitating teenage scorn perfectly. 'Besides,' she went on, hiding a smile at his snort of disgust, 'it wasn't the wine that made me dance—it was the music. I just love Strauss!' She managed a dreamy smile, desperate that he shouldn't suspect the devastating effect that evening had had on her.

Jesse's eyes crinkled at the corners and he smiled softly at her. 'It was rather—magical, wasn't it?'

Such simple words, so easily spoken, but they had a heady effect on her. Her heart sang. He had felt it too. Hastily she began to pack away the lunch, hiding her delight from him.

'I would have thought your tastes would run more in line with Kiss or some other rock group,' Jesse continued as he helped her pack away the lunch.

'Oh, they do! I love music of any kind. Don't you?' she asked, deftly folding the blanket and stuffing it into the knapsack, still keeping her too revealing face averted.

'I doubt that my tastes are quite as—catholic—as yours,' he said, taking the knapsack from her as they left. 'And I don't usually haul my stereo equipment with me when I'm on holiday.'

'Well, there was no point in leaving it in storage, was there? Besides,' she continued, sounding slightly wistful, 'it's good company.'

'Music and a cat,' he said as they trudged through the sand. 'Is that all the company you need?'

'No,' she said, turning her green eyes directly on him. 'Will you come for supper tomorrow?'

Jesse threw back his head and shouted with laughter. 'Been feeling lonely, have you? Okay, I'll come, but it'll have to be early evening. I'm going out on the boat with Tom, but we expect to be back before dark.'

'Great!' said Stefanie, unable to prevent a happy smile. 'I'll make something that'll keep if you're later than you expect.'

He smiled down at her. 'Well, little girl,' he drawled, 'if you can make a meal to match that apple pie you made the other day, it'll be worth an evening of Strauss and Kiss!'

Feeling buoyant and slightly giddy, Stefanie stuck her tongue out at him and ran laughing down the path beating him back to the truck.

Stefanie found herself waiting impatiently from about four o'clock on. Everything was ready early. She had made a beef stew, hearty with chunky meat and vegetables, and its rich aroma filled the kitchen as it simmered on the back burner. Feeling Jesse had dropped enough hints about it yesterday, she made an apple pie for dessert. It was a simple meal that should appeal to a man who had worked all day in the brisk ocean air.

Choosing an outfit for the evening wasn't as easy a decision. Jeans and cords were definitely out, and most of her good clothes were just too sophisticated for who she was supposed to be. Finally, she drew a pair of lounging pyjamas from the closet, eyeing them doubtfully. The pale green silk was a perfect foil for her colouring and she loved the Oriental cut, but . . .

'No buts? They're perfect,' she told herself with more than a hint of anger. The ridiculous charade had gone on long enough. She wasn't going to play the wide-eyed ingénue to his self-appointed role as mentor any longer. Stefanie winced as she remembered how she had gambolled about on the beach yesterday. 'And all those cutesy remarks about Daddy!' she groaned. Determined to be herself tonight, consequences be damned, she began to dress.

Later, as she stood fully dressed in front of the mirror, she felt her resolve slip. With the carefully applied make-up and softly cascading hair, she no longer looked like a teenager, and suddenly she knew she had to avoid a direct confrontation with Jesse. She reached for a tissue and quickly removed most of the make-up, then she pulled her hair into one long braid down her back. She stared critically at her reflection.

'That's more like it—little girl,' she said sarcastically, and muttering at her cowardice, went downstairs to wait.

Time dragged. Would he never come? Stefanie was very much on edge, both in anticipation of the evening ahead and at the lengths she was willing to take her deception.

There was no fooling herself as to why. There was only one reason for not having told Jesse the truth long before now. Purely and simply put, the lie served as protection.

Jesse stirred something in her, feelings that had lain dormant since Dawson's hateful attack all those years ago. Until Jesse she had existed in a kind of sexual limbo, subconsciously believing that it had been her innocent response to Dawson's kisses that had been the root of his brutal attempt at rape. The subliminal message had been obeyed. Desire was suppressed.

Stefanie sat before the fire, slender fingers clasped around one knee, gazing reflectively into the flames. She had always avoided men like Jesse before. She had men as friends, men who were witty and charming—and perfectly willing to let her set the limits, always very platonic, in their relationships with her.

Jesse was not that kind of man. Stefanie's slowly awakening desires could sense a strong and sensual man under the casual manner he had adopted with her. The same manner, she thought with a smile, that undoubtedly protected him from the amorous crushes of half his female students!

And it was that very attitude, in deference to the tender age he believed her to be, that had allowed Stefanie to relax her guard. With her defences down, his vibrancy had penetrated her barriers.

I like him, Stefanie mused with a smile. I like him a lot. With a flash of guilt, she was reminded again of the lie she was living. I must tell him, she thought with fresh determination. Maybe he won't be angry. Maybe, she thought wistfully, he'll be—glad!

She sighed softly as she poked absently at the fire. The truth would allow their friendship to develop—but could she handle anything more? And why was she so sure he would really care? She remembered Louisa with a grimace.

She stirred restlessly, catching a glimpse of the clock with a start. Jesse could arrive at any moment. Jumping up, she threw another log on the fire and put on some unobtrusive music, determined to be in a less introverted frame of mind when he got there. She was in the kitchen stirring the stew when the back door opened.

'Aha! Just as I thought—unlocked!'

Stefanie drew a deep breath and managed an almost bright smile. 'Just who do you think is going to come anyway? This isn't exactly downtown Vancouver!'

'Can't be too careful,' Jesse said, wagging a warning finger. He shrugged off his coat and sniffed the air. 'Smells fantastic,' he remarked, lifting the cover from the simmering pot. 'Stew will be perfect after the day I've had—was it cold out there!'

Stefanie took his jacket and went to hang it on a hook by the door. In her vulnerable frame of mind, she was acutely conscious of him, of the energy he exuded. She knew with certainly that in this fragile state she couldn't tell him the truth. Not tonight. It would have to be as Aggie suggested.

She caught Jesse's look as she turned. He was frowning slightly as he looked at her and she was sure she saw concern in his eyes. She smiled at him, a lovely open smile, her eyes soft for an instant with the pleasure she felt at having him here. 'I hope you're hungry,' she said lightly, 'or I'll be eating left over stew for a week.'

'I'm starving,' he said with a smile, and added softly, 'Are you okay, Stef?'

'I'm beginning to think I just may be,' she answered, and his frown deepened. Before he could say anything, she placed a light hand on his arm, smiling up at him. 'Come through to the fire,' she said, leading the way. 'Would you like some wine? It's all I have.'

'Yes, my little wino, I know,' Jesse teased as he held up the bottle to read the label. 'I see your father has good taste in wine.'

'My father?' She had almost forgotten. 'Why—why are you so sure I didn't choose it myself?'

'Because, little girl,' he said with a sardonic smile, 'your age group invariably chooses one of the sweet soda pop varieties—you know, the ones named after cute little animals.'

Stefanie suppressed a sigh. Was he so blind? She raised her glass to her lips and looked at him over the rim. 'Maybe I have more mature tastes,' she murmured with a hint of seriousness underlying the coyness in her voice.

'Maybe you do, little girl, maybe you do,' Jesse drawled, studying her face with an intentness she found disturbing. Hastily she moved towards the fire.

'Aren't there any chairs in this place?' Jesse asked, lowering himself on to a pile of cushions. 'This business of sitting on the floor is harder on older bones!'

'I find it quite comfortable myself.' Stefanie dropped gracefully down beside him.

'Ah, yes,' he said, 'but then you're not thirty-five!'

'Thirty-five!' She exclaimed with a nasty note of incredulousness. 'That old?'

'Yes, little girl—that old!' His smile mocked her. 'I even have grey hair—want to see?' His grey eyes gleamed derisively as he bent his head towards her.

Knowing it was the last thing he would expect, and quite unable to resist, Stefanie reached out to lightly stroke the gold-tipped curls. 'You're right,' she teased before leaning back against the cushions. 'Lots!'

His eyes narrowed as they looked at her with an intentness even more unnerving than before. 'Put there, no doubt,' he said with deliberate slowness,' through my dealings with precocious little schoolgirls!' And then, dropping the subject, he asked with a smile, 'Is supper ready yet?'

'I'll check,' Stefanie said, hiding her amusement as she scrambled up. He had certainly sounded like a schoolteacher just then, she thought with a grimace as she went quickly into the kitchen. I think I've just been told to behave myself!

Once again she felt an overwhelming curiosity to know how he would act towards her if he knew her actual age. As she busied herself with the final preparations, she knew that she was through with playing seventeen. She would avoid telling him the truth, for tonight anyway, but the role playing was definitely over. Let him puzzle it out.

Determinedly she set the food on the table and went into the living room. She watched Jesse for a moment as he sat staring into the fire, the flames highlighting his strong features. His brows were drawn together with a frown and Stefanie knew, with a smile, that he had noticed the change in her. 'It's ready,' she called softly. 'Let's eat.'

Jesse smiled at her as he raised himself from the floor. 'Coming, little girl,' he drawled.

She felt a spurt of exasperation. She whirled around and stood before him, hand on outflung hip, the green light of her eyes flashing. 'Do me a favour,' she demanded. 'Stop calling me little girl—I'm not, you know!'

Jesse stood still, his smoky eyes narrow as they met her defiant look. Then he dropped his eyes from her face to rove with slow study over her body, alluringly draped with green silk. His smile was ironic as he raised his eyes to hers once more. 'No, Stefanie,' he said, 'I guess you're not.'

The flush that had stained her cheeks during his slow appraisal was not caused by embarrassment. It was need. For a breath-stopping instant she had wanted nothing more than to feel his arms around her, to feel the strong crush of his chest against her tingling breasts as his lips claimed hers in a kiss that could only burn. Biting her lip, she turned away quickly, hiding her desire from him. 'Let's eat,' she said abruptly.

The meal was hot and savoury. Jesse ate with hungry gusto, but Stefanie could only manage to nibble at her portion. Their conversation was light and friendly, but she found herself too overwhelmingly aware of him to have much appetite—for food anyway, she had to acknowledge with a flash of humour.

Jesse declined dessert, saying he would have it later with coffee, and at her insistence went into the living room while she cleared up. She needed the breathing space.

Jesse had built up the fire to a roaring blaze and lay stretched out full length with a pile of cushions to prop him up. The cat lay on its back beside him, one hind leg twitching with pleasure as Jesse absently scratched its chin. Lucky cat, Stefanie thought as she watched him

for a moment. Her eyes absorbed the lean length of his
body, the broad expanse of his shoulders ... She
sighed and shrugged before going over to the stereo to
put an André Gagnon album on to the turntable.

Jesse seemed disinclined to talk, merely smiling at her
as she sat down opposite him. Sensing that he wanted
to relax after a full meal, Stefanie stared quietly into the
flames, slowly relaxing as she became absorbed in the
music. As she enjoyed the sensuous expertise of the
pianist and his musicians she drifted into a light and
dreamy sleep.

As her eyes fluttered open she saw Jesse sitting beside
her, a soft and gentle look in his eyes. 'And you're trying
to tell me you're not a little girl,' he murmured softly,
brushing a strand of hair from her flushed cheek. For a
moment their eyes met, and as hers smiled warmly she
could see the perplexity in his. And then the shutter
dropped.

He stood up abruptly and walked towards the
kitchen. 'I'll be right back,' he called over his shoulder,
stilling her fears that perhaps he had decided it would
be best for him to leave.

In minutes he was back carrying a brown leather
case. 'I hope you've rested sufficiently to be able to
meet the challenge.'

'Challenge? What challenge?' Stefanie sat up and
stretched lazily.

'Backgammon,' he said, opening the case and setting
up the board on the floor beside him.

'You're on!' Stefanie moved over quickly to sit cross-
legged on the other side of the board.

He raised an eyebrow. 'I take it you've played before?'

'Oh—once or twice,' she replied, her bright look of
interest belying her offhand words.

'Mmmm,' he said 'we'll see about that.' He rolled the
dice to begin the game.

Almost two hours later they played a final game to
break the deadlock. Jesse managed to capture one of
her men and three rolls later won the game.

'Sheer luck,' Stefanie muttered, stretching her long
legs to relieve cramped muscles.

'Luck nothing,' he grinned at her. 'Pure skill.'

'Skill!' she snorted. 'Hah!'

Jesse laughed at her, snapping the case shut. 'Don't be such a sore loser—you'll have me calling you little girl again!' He turned so that his next words were almost lost. 'I'd almost forgotten as it was.'

She had forgotten the charade herself. For that brief interlude she had forgotten everything but the pleasure of his company. She had relished the sound of his low chuckles, the sight of his lean hands as they moved the backgammon pieces around the board. 'Jesse——' She started to tell him, but the words stuck in her throat. Sick at her cowardice, she stood up. 'I—I'll make coffee,' she said hastily, and hurried through to the kitchen.

She watched him as he ate a piece of pie, chatting nervously to cover telling silences. He would be going soon and she knew with certainty that she didn't want him to leave. She wanted to spend the night in his arms, to have him teach her the joys of making love. She was strongly aware of a growing confidence that she could respond to his demands, that she could return his kisses and caresses until—the rawness of her thoughts made her gasp.

Jesse was watching her closely. 'Is there something wrong?' he asked.

'No—no, nothing's wrong,' she answered with a wry little laugh. 'The—the coffee is too hot.' They finished in silence.

'Well,' said Jesse, pushing his chair back, 'I've got to be going.' His voice seemed hesitant as though he too was reluctant to end the evening.

Stefanie waited by the door as he put on his coat, biting her bottom lip in a vain attempt to still the tensions welling in her, unable to look at him.

'Stefanie,' he began, and when she refused to look up, raised her head with gentle fingers under her chin. 'What's wrong?'

Stefanie stared into his eyes, saw concern and puzzlement mixed, and some deeper emotion that somehow invited her trust. 'Nothing,' she said, relaxing perceptively. Her mouth softened and widened into a lovely smile. 'There's nothing wrong with me!' The words came out with such joy and certainty that he was puzzled even further, searching her face as though to find clues.

Still smiling, her eyes luminous in her flushed face, Stefanie reached up to smooth the tangle of beard around his firm lips. He pulled her hand away with a firm grip, his eyes darkening with warning. Before he could speak, she stood on tiptoe and put her soft mouth to his, catching him by surprise. She felt his control slip, felt a shudder run through him as his arms tightened, pulling her against his hard length, and she trembled with the shock waves of desire that flashed through her. Just as her lips parted under his, inviting deeper caresses, he pushed her away so abruptly she almost lost her balance. As she reached for the doorframe to steady herself, she felt a fleeting finger trace down her cheek. Looking up quickly, she met his eyes just as a shutter dropped, effectively concealing himself from her.

'Jesse, it's okay. I'm not . . .'

'No, it's not okay,' he interrupted coldly, and added with deliberate emphasis, 'Goodnight—little girl.'

'But I'm not! I . . .'

But he was already out of the door. Stefanie ran out after him. 'Jesse!' she called to his retreating figure. 'Jesse!' He disappeared into the moonlit night.

'Damn it!' She stormed back into the kitchen, slamming the door shut behind her in pure frustration. She flung herself around the room slamming cupboards and drawers, enraged with the charade that had gone too far.

'Oh, why did I start this ridiculous thing in the first place?' she moaned. Throwing her hands up in disgust, she continued to bang around the kitchen, putting dishes away with a force that left them rattling on the shelves.

'That's it!' she declared to the cat, who sat blinking, disturbed by all the racket. 'I'll tell him the truth tomorrow. No more little girl!' she vowed bitterly.

She was far too fidgety to do much more than wander from room to room. Maybe a bath would help, she thought restlessly, and took a mystery book upstairs with her, intending to dull her senses with escapism and hot water.

The bath was no help. The musky perfume of the bath oil and the silkiness of the hot water on her sensitive limbs tantalised her already heightened senses. She sat up in the tub, throwing her book on the floor in disgust. I think a cold shower would have been a better idea, she thought sarcastically. What she was feeling was pure sexual desire flamed by Jesse's kiss.

Jesse's kiss? she asked herself, reaching down to pull the plug. Just who was it who did all the kissing? But there had been a response—his cool lips had warmed and softened under the touch of her mouth. Stefanie sighed and pulled the shower curtain shut, hoping fervently that his withdrawal had been because of her supposed youth and not lack of interest. She stepped under the cool spray.

First thing in the morning, she promised herself, I'm going over to straighten things out. Nothing further could be resolved until the truth was known. Determinedly, she put it out of her mind, stepped out of the shower and dried herself vigorously.

Feeling chilled, she slipped into a soft white flannel nightgown, rather Victorian in style with a high lace-trimmed neck and long puffy sleeves, the full length brushing against the floor as she walked. She decided bed would be a good place to read the book that promised to be suspenseful, and quickly ran downstairs to let the cat out. Knowing he would want in before morning, she opened the window in the utility room just wide enough for him to squeeze through. Then she dashed back upstairs, jumped into bed and snuggled under the blankets, book in one hand, apple in the other.

It was close to two hours later when she finally gave up the battle against sleep. Yawning, she put the book down and turned out the bedside light, falling quickly to sleep.

Stefanie sat up in bed. What had wakened her? She pushed the heavy hair back from her face and listened closely. There it was again! A loud thud sounded from the kitchen. 'Stupid cat,' she muttered sleepily, and lay down again. As she rolled over on to her side, her knee came into contact with a soft lump in the middle of the bed. About the size of . . . She reached out and touched soft silky fur.

If that's the cat, she thought, lying perfectly still, then what—who is down there? Fear rushed through her, leaving a tingling metallic taste in its wake. Oh God, I forgot to lock the door!

Crash! The loud noise of something breaking sent her flying out of bed. Panic coursed through her and pictures from the book she had been engrossed in loomed large and vivid in the darkness of the room. Escape became her prime concern. She could hear more banging, things breaking in the kitchen. Whoever it was was being very destructive and would probably become violent if a witness was discovered. Stefanie willed reluctant legs to move towards the stairs. With caution controlling every movement, she inched her way, trying hard to ignore the urge to run heedlessly from the house.

Holding her breath, she slid the glass patio doors open inch by cautious inch, listening with taut nerves to the sounds of destruction coming from the kitchen. And then, suddenly, the noise stopped. Terrified that this must mean the intruder was on his way to the rest of the house, Stefanie squeezed through the narrow opening and ran out into the night.

Without thought, she fled in the direction of Jesse's house and stumbled sobbing, nearly out of control, along the path. The waning moon cast barely enough light to prevent her from colliding into the stumps and roots that made the trail so attractive in daylight. She ran as though a thousand devils were flying close behind, her bare feet scratched and bruised.

Finally she could see a light shining through the trees and with a glad cry increased her speed. The ducks and geese in the yard echoed her terror as she fled ghost-like past their enclosure. Sobbing with relief, she ran on to the porch and flung herself inside.

'Jesse,' she called. Where was he? 'Jesse!' she called again more desperately. *'Jesse!'* Her voice ended on a note that was almost a scream.

'Stefanie!' Jesse stepped into the room, a towel wrapped around his waist, his hair and beard dripping water from the shower. He stared at her as she stood barefoot in her white gown, hair tumbled in wild confusion about her face—a face that was as white as the gown. 'My God, Stefanie—what's happened?'

Stefanie could only stare at him, at the hard beauty of his nearly naked body. All the desires of earlier came rushing back intensified, ruthlessly casting fear aside.

'What's happened!' He gripped her shoulders in his strong hands, frowning with puzzled concern.

'I—I . . .' She tried to speak, but couldn't think past the touch of his hands on her shoulders. She shook her head, amazed that after such terror all she could feel now was the flood of desire the sight, the fresh smell of his body caused. She licked her lips with nervous agitation and, with what seemed like great physical effort, dragged her eyes from his body to meet his puzzled eyes.

'Stefanie? What is it?' He shook her gently. 'Tell me!'

Stefanie drew a deep breath and tried to pull herself together. 'Th-there's s-someone in the—the house.'

'Who—is it a burglar?'

'I—I don't know,' she stammered. 'I was sleeping. There were noises from downstairs—things breaking, and it wasn't the c-cat. I w-went out the side door.' She shuddered violently with the turmoil of mixed emotions running through her.

'Come and sit down,' Jesse said kindly, leading her to a chair near the fireplace. He took a thick woollen sweater from the back of the couch and draped it over her trembling shoulders.

He stood in front of her wearing nothing but the towel that barely covered his narrow hips. Stefanie stared at his wide shoulders, his smooth chest and slowly lowered her eyes to his flat hard stomach. She clenched her fingers to prevent them from reaching out with a will of their own and plucking the towel from the leanly muscled thighs with their sprinkling of dark curly hair.

With a moan she hoped he would think was uttered with the remnants of fear, she hid her face in her hands, striving desperately for control.

'I'll get dressed,' said Jesse, laying light fingers on her silky hair. 'You're safe now.'

Safe! Stefanie had never felt less safe in her life. For the first time in many years, her control was slipping, leaving her with a sense of panic that had nothing to do with the intruder. Rising from the chair, she paced the floor rapidly. Maybe I've stayed here long enough, she thought heavily. She felt a sudden longing to be back at work, immersed in the soothing logic of accounting; to be back in a routine with less time left for idle fantasies; to be back in control. With great effort she managed to pull herself into some semblance of control, and by the time Jesse returned, clad in jeans and a red-checkered flannel shirt, she felt calmer.

'I phoned the R.C.M.P. detachment—they'll have someone over there soon,' he said. 'You stay here—I'll go see what's going on.'

'I'm not staying.'

'Stay,' he coaxed. 'I'll bring some shoes and a coat back for you. You'll freeze going out like that again.'

'I'm coming.' She was adamant. 'Let's go,' she said, and slipped her arms into the sweater.

Jesse shrugged. 'Suit yourself—but stay back when we get there.'

They followed the path at a quieter pace than Stefanie's headlong flight, and she was glad of the warm comfort of his hand holding hers. Soon they could see the house looming in the clearing, dark and almost foreboding.

'Be careful,' she whispered nervously as Jesse left her at the edge of the yard to slip in through the door she had left open. A moment later a car drew up silently in the drive, lights out. The police. Stefanie followed the line of trees until she stood by the car.

'Jesse's in there,' she told the constable in a low voice.

He nodded silently, already going to the back door. Suddenly the lights in the kitchen blazed on. Stefanie stifled a scream of surprise and then sagged with relief. Jesse couldn't have found anyone there if he thought it safe to turn on the lights.

She walked as quickly as her aching bare feet would allow, anxious to join the men—then stopped abruptly at the sound of loud laughter coming from within. Laughter? She hurried through the door.

The two men stood amid a litter of broken dishes, torn and scattered cereal boxes and the thin layer of flour that covered everything, laughing uproariously. They tried unsuccessfully to stop when they saw Stefanie standing in the doorway looking totally bewildered.

'Wha . . .?' she began.

'Er—we think we know who the intruder was,' Jesse told her, his eyes alight with suppressed laughter. 'Usually wears a black mask over his eyes, short and furry, weighs about twenty-five pounds—and has a bushy striped tail.'

Short? Furry? Stephanie looked from one man to another, comprehension slowly dawning. 'You mean . . .?'

'A raccoon,' Jesse supplied with a wide grin.

She sat down heavily at the table. All that over a raccoon! She dropped her forehead to the palm of her hand. A raccoon! She turned her head to look at the men. It was obvious that they found the whole thing hilarious, although the young constable was doing his best not to let it show. 'And I've never been so frightened in my life!' she groaned. Then slowly she began to see the humour of the situation. Her colour returned and her face lit up with a beautiful smile. 'That does it!' she stated firmly. 'I'm going to stop reading myself to sleep with murder mysteries!' Released from her fear, she began to laugh.

'Well,' she said finally, looking around with a grimace, 'I've got to get this cleaned up—any volunteers?' she added hopefully.

'Put the coffee on, Stef,' said Jesse, reaching for the broom. 'I'll give you a hand. We'll excuse Jim, though.'

'No problem,' said Jim. 'I'll just radio dispatch and let them know what's going on—be right back.'

Later, the three of them sat with pie and coffee in the freshly scrubbed kitchen. 'I'm starting to feel pretty silly,' Stefanie admitted.

'Don't worry about it,' Jim said seriously, as he stirred his coffee. 'You did the right thing. If there had been someone down here you might have been badly hurt. Getting out was the best thing to do in the circumstances.'

'I suppose,' Stefanie agreed. 'Still, I'm surprised that a wild animal would come into the house like that.'

'It was probably tame at one time,' said Jesse, pushing his empty plate away. 'People make pets out of them when they're babies—they're quite irresistible then. But they can become a nuisance when they get older, so they're often released back into the wild. And,' he added, 'with no fear of humans, they can become quite troublesome.'

'You're telling me!' Stefanie rose to clear the table as the two men made to leave.

'I'll drop you off, Jess,' said Jim, replacing his cap on his fair head. 'Goodnight, Stefanie,' he said with a warm smile in his hazel eyes. 'Don't hesitate to call me if there's another problem.'

'I won't, Jim. And thanks very much—especially for not being put out by all this.' She smiled sincerely at him.

'No problem,' he said, and left with a casual wave.

'He wouldn't consider it a problem if you called him to change a light bulb,' Jesse murmured wickedly. 'He's smitten.'

'Oh, do you really think so?' asked Stefanie with wide-eyed pleasure. 'He's cute!' she added with deliberate enthusiasm.

'And not a grey hair on his fair head,' Jesse mocked, bending down to drop a light kiss on her cheek. 'Go to bed, little girl. And lock the door!' With that he was gone into the night.

Stefanie shut the door behind him, leaning against it for a long moment. She had run the gamut of emotions tonight and was suddenly overcome by a deep weariness. Stumbling slightly, she went upstairs to bed. Hugging Jesse's sweater tightly around her, she fell into a deep dreamless sleep.

CHAPTER SIX

JESSE'S sweater provided the perfect excuse for Stefanie to go over to his place the next morning. Somewhere along the course of last night's events, she had resolved that the truth must be told. She would procrastinate no longer.

Dressing carefully but casually in khaki slacks and a creamy angora sweater, she applied a light touch of make-up and left her hair in a silken fall on her shoulders. Perhaps she didn't look that much older than the teenager he thought she was, but all she wanted at the moment was for him to hear her out—and try to understand.

Apprehensively she walked the path between the two houses, clutching his sweater against her chest as if it was some sort of talisman that would protect her from his undoubted anger. The birds were still in their pen as she passed by them and up the stairs to knock on the door. There was no answer, and swallowing nervously, Stefanie knocked again. It was not Jesse who answered the door.

'Yes?' asked a sleepy-eyed blonde through the narrow crack of open door.

Blinking rapidly in surprise, Stefanie struggled to collect herself. 'I—I just came to return Jesse's sweater.' Her voice was thin with dismay. This was no casual visitor. All the woman wore was a man's red-checkered flannel shirt unbuttoned to such an extent that it barely covered her voluptuous curves. It was Jesse's shirt.

'I'll take it—Jesse's just getting up,' she said with a sleepy yawn. 'We didn't get much sleep last night.'

The contented smile on her pretty face told Stefanie just how satisfying that lack of sleep had been.

'Louisa?' called Jesse's voice from another room. 'Who is it?'

Startled, Stefanie thrust the sweater at the other

90

woman. 'Tell him thanks,' she managed to mumble, and hurried down the stairs and out of sight among the trees.

Louisa's here, she thought dully. She was beginning to realise the full implications of what she had just seen. The intimacy that Aggie had hinted at was obviously true. That sleep-tussled hair, the half-buttoned shirt and especially that contented little smile—all dead give-aways, Stefanie thought with growing dejection.

Reaching her place, she went straight to her car and was soon on the highway. The sight of Louisa in the doorway had been shocking—her obvious disarray doubly so. Stefanie felt a flash of anger—at Jesse, but more so with herself, for allowing her emotions to tie in with a man who was obviously attached elsewhere. Very attached, she thought gloomily, and turned off the highway to park.

She sat lost in thought. It was perfectly clear to her now that all those little lies and deceptions about her age, played to keep her safe, had been totally unnecessary; that all his attentions had truly been made out of kindness and nothing more. There had been no need to enmesh herself in deceit—he would never have been interested in her other than as an amusing diversion in the first place!

Stefanie groaned with an element of pain and got out of the car. She followed a steep path that wound down a steep hill to a sandy beach. Clouds hung low, swollen with rain. Scattered wisps of mist clung to holes and crevices in the black rocks that outlined the sand. The sullen day suited her mood and she trudged along the water's edge despondently kicking a bit of shell before her.

So much for thinking he had held off last night because of my age! she thought miserably. Obviously he had been looking forward to Louisa's visit. Well, she decided with a shrug, it could have been worse—she could have been there when I ran over last night scared out of my tree by a racoon! With a rather grim smile she scrambled over the rocks that separated one beach from another. Deserting the sand for the logs, she jumped from one to another, leaping farther and faster until one poorly balanced giant brought her down with a thud. Panting, she sat where she had fallen.

What difference would knowing her true age really make to Jesse? she wondered. Before this morning Louisa had been a vague threat somewhere over in Vancouver, and it had been easy to imagine Jesse's pleasure when he realised just how much older she was. But now, with the clear picture of Louisa in her mind, charmingly dishevelled from a night in Jesse's bed, Stefanie found her hopes for Jesse returning her interest taking a dismal plunge. She stared moodily out over the grey water.

Maybe, she thought later with a glimmer of renewed hope, I could give Louisa a run for her money. The question was—would Jesse be interested? Something inside her shouted yes! No matter who had started that kiss last night, she hadn't been the only one to respond—she didn't need a whole lot of experience to realise that. Was it her age or Louisa that prompted his withdrawal? Stefanie sighed. No doubt about it—she wouldn't know any more than she did now until Jesse saw her as the woman she was. She had given him a few clues last night, but come Tom's party she would give him the full show. Tossing her head with determination, Stefanie began the walk back. She wasn't going to give up—she hadn't even started yet!

To her surprise she saw a strange car in her driveway. Puzzled as to whom it belonged, she got out of her car just as the owner came round from the front of the house.

'Stefanie!' he called.

'Hi, Jim,' Stefanie smiled at the young constable of last night as he came towards her.

His smile was friendly and his hazel eyes regarded her with frank admiration. 'I came over to see if everything was all right after last night—any more problems with the masked bandit?'

'None,' Stefanie grinned. 'I'm keeping the window in the utility room closed—no matter how many times I have to open the door for that cat!' She fumbled in her pocket for the key. 'Would you like to come in for coffee?' It would be nice to think about someone other than Jesse.

'Love to,' Jim said promptly, and followed her in.

'Sit down—won't be a minute.' Stefanie busied herself with the coffee-maker. 'Are you off duty today?'

He nodded as he sat down at the table. 'I hope you don't mind me dropping in like this.'

Stefanie smiled and shook her head. 'Not at all, Jim—believe me! Apart from Jesse, you're the only person I've seen all week. I'm glad of the company.'

'I thought you might be over at Jess's this morning,' Jim admitted, smiling his thanks as she placed a mug of coffee in front of him.

'I did go over earlier to—to return something,' she acknowledged, 'but I didn't stay. He's got company,' she added in a murmur, looking down at the table.

Jim nodded. 'Louisa. Yes, I know. She got there just after I drove Jess home last night—she must have taken the last ferry. Guess she'll be staying for a few days.'

Stefanie listened to his words with a sinking heart. She desperately wanted to see Jesse, to talk to him and try to explain why she had let the lie go on for so long, but not while his—his lover was staying with him! With an effort, she turned her attention back to Jim.

'I saw Tom just before coming out,' he was saying. 'He asked me to let you know that his engagement party is Friday night.'

Stefanie stifled a sigh. That would have been exciting news if Louisa hadn't shown up! Undoubtedly, she would accompany Jesse to the party. Still, she managed a smile and said, 'Good. I've been looking forward to it. I'm more than ready for a bit of socialising.'

'Say, Stefanie, will you—that is, if you don't have other plans—will you come with me?' Jim's fair face flushed slightly.

Stefanie didn't have to think twice. 'Yes, Jim, I will. Thanks for asking.'

'It's my pleasure!' he grinned at her in his friendly way. He finished the rest of his coffee and after a few moments of talk, stood up to leave. 'See you Friday night, then—about eight?'

'I'll be ready,' she promised, feeling a twinge of guilt. Nice as he was, it wasn't Jim she was going to be ready for.

Stefanie spent the days before the dance in a tense state. Jesse didn't come over, which wasn't really surprising considering Louisa's visit. She had seen the two of them on the beach one morning and had managed to duck out of sight behind the trees. Louisa's hand was tucked under Jesse's arm as they strolled along, and Stefanie had watched how Jesse's face lit up as he smiled down on the pretty upturned face of his companion. She had watched with tear-blurred eyes as Jesse lowered his head to kiss Louisa, and then, unable to bear any more, fled.

Friday finally arrived. Stefanie was nervously excited, feeling like a high-school girl getting ready for her first prom. I think I'm going through a delayed adolescence, she thought with somewhat exasperated amusement as she waved her hands in the air to dry the coat of bronze-coloured nail polish. Where was all that cool sophistication she had been so proud of? Shaking her head in disgust, she went up to shower.

Afterwards, she slipped into a short white terry robe and began to towel-dry her hair. There was an unexpected knock at the door. Stefanie tightened the sash on the robe and ran downstairs to answer it. If that's Jim, she thought, frowning slightly, he's far too early!

'Jesse!' Stefanie clutched her robe tighter and stepped back in surprise.

'Hi, little girl,' he drawled with his lopsided grin, and came in shutting the door behind him. 'Not ready yet, I see.'

'Jesse—I didn't expect to see you. I——' She stopped, confused by his presence, by the look she saw on his face as he ran his eyes over her damp figure, lingering noticeably on the smooth expanse of her legs, visible to mid-thigh.

His eyes darkened. 'Get dressed,' he said brusquely.

'No hurry,' Stefanie said with asperity, annoyed that he had taken so much for granted. 'My date doesn't get here until eight.'

Jesse raised his eyebrows and looked at her with more than a hint of surprise visible in his eyes. 'Date?'

'Mm, yes—Jim's taking me.' Now over the shock of his unexpected appearance, Stefanie felt a growing amusement. Had that been a flash of consternation in those smoky eyes? 'What about you? Aren't you taking your—er—house guest?' she asked sweetly.

'Louisa left last night,' he replied rather shortly. He ran his fingers through his curls, a frown marking his forehead. 'I guess I just assumed we'd go together.'

'Jim didn't assume—he asked,' said Stefanie with a pert grin. She opened the door. 'Now, if you don't mind?' Biting back a smile, she watched him leave. 'Don't worry,' she called after him, 'I'll save you a dance!'

Louisa was gone! Stefanie fairly danced back upstairs, giggling to herself until she remembered that the second surprise she had in store for Jesse tonight would undoubtedly cause more than a frown. Somewhat sobered by the thought of what lay ahead, she dressed for the party.

She was more than a little satisfied with the image she saw when she finally stood before the mirror. No one could possibly mistake the woman reflected there for a 'little girl'. She wore a flattering jumpsuit in a fine cottony material, the black background faintly traced with a leafy gold pattern. It was cuffed at the ankles as well as the wrists and the blouson top was unbuttoned just enough for a glimpse of the lacy black camisole that delicately covered the creamy swell of her breasts. Her hair curled softly back from her wide forehead to tumble down her back in ruby ripples. But it was the make-up that made the real difference. Skilful use of shadow, liner and mascara elongated her eyes, making them less round and guileless. A light foundation covered her freckles and a careful dusting of blush heightened her cheekbones and her face at once became more classically sculptured. The pretty girl had become a beautiful woman.

She quickly fastened a ropey gold chain around her throat, slipped into high heels, and as a final touch, used a musky perfume. As ready as she would ever be, she went downstairs to wait for Jim.

Fortunately, he was a little early. Just as Stefanie thought her nerves couldn't take any more waiting, she heard his car pull up in the drive.

'Jim,' she said warmly as she opened the door. 'Come in.'

'Thanks, Stefanie,' he said. 'Hey, you look great! No, wait. I take that back—you're absolutely stunning!' He had a slightly incredulous look as he stared at her transformation.

'Thank you, Jim.' She accepted his compliment with a smile. He looked—nice. He wore a neat brown jacket with tan slacks and his short fair hair was neatly styled. 'I'm ready,' she smiled brightly, thrusting visions of gold-tipped black curls aside. 'Shall we leave now?'

'Might as well,' said Jim. 'There'll be a lot of people tonight and I'd like to get a good table—next to the dance floor!' he added with a grin. He helped her into a short black bouclé jacket that fastened with a wide belt, and ushered her to his car.

The parking lot in front of the tiny hall was full, and as Stefanie walked into the room full of strangers, she was doubly glad of Jim's presence. As he took her jacket to the cloakroom, Tom came towards her.

'Hi, Tom!' she said brightly.

'Stefanie!' Tom's dark eyes sparkled and he grinned at her. 'You're looking good tonight.'

'Thanks, Tom,' Stefanie smiled, instantly at ease with the friendly man. 'You don't look so bad yourself,' she added, admiring his well cut sand-coloured suit. 'Is Aggie here yet?'

'Jesse is going to bring her over later,' Tom explained. 'She tires easily these days and didn't want to come too early.'

Jesse wasn't here yet. Stefanie relaxed perceptibly, glad the confrontation had been postponed a while

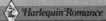

LOVE BEYOND REASON
There was a surprise in store for Amy!

Amy had thought nothing could be as perfect as the days she had shared with Vic Hoyt in New York City—before he took off for his Peace Corps assignment in Kenya.

Impulsively, Amy decided to follow. She was shocked to find Vic established in his new life... and interested in a new girl friend.

Amy faced a choice: be smart and go home... or stay and fight for the only man she would ever love.

MAN OF POWER
Sara took her role seriously

Although Sara had already planned her escape from the subservient position in which her father's death had placed her, Morgan Haldane's timely appearance had definitely made it easier.

All Morgan had asked in return was that she pose as his fiancée. He'd confessed to needing protection from his partner's wife, Louise, and that part of Sara's job proved easy.

But unfortunately for Sara's heart, Morgan hadn't told her about Monique...

Your Romantic Adventure Starts Here.

THE LEO MAN
"He's every bit as sexy as his father!"

Her grandmother thought that description would appeal to Rowan, but Rowan was determined to avoid any friendship with the arrogant James Fraser.

Aboard his luxury yacht, that wasn't easy. When they were all shipwrecked on a tropical island, it proved impossible.

And besides, if it weren't for James, none of them would be alive. Rowan was confused. Was it merely gratitude that she now felt for this strong and rugged man?

THE WINDS OF WINTER
She'd had so much— now she had nothing

Anne didn't dwell on it, but the pain was still with her—the double-edged pain of grief and rejection.

It had greatly altered her; Anne barely resembled the girl who four years earlier had left her husband, David. He probably wouldn't even recognize her—especially with another name.

Anne made up her mind. She just *had* to go to his house to discover if what she suspected was true...

These FOUR free Harlequin Romance novels allow you to enter the world of romance, love and desire. As a member of the Harlequin Home Subscription Plan, you can continue to experience all the moods of love. You'll be inspired by moments so real. . .so moving. . .you won't want them to end. So start your own Harlequin Romance adventure by returning the reply card below. DO IT TODAY!

BUSINESS REPLY CARD

First Class   Permit No. 70   Tempe, AZ

POSTAGE WILL BE PAID BY ADDRESSEE

**Harlequin Reader Service
2504 W. Southern Avenue,
Tempe, Arizona 85282**

NO POSTAGE
NECESSARY
IF MAILED
IN THE
UNITED STATES

longer. She chatted comfortably with Tom, waiting for
Jim, when they were joined by a pretty, dark-haired
young woman wearing a vivid red dress.

'This is Rose,' said Tom with a note of pride in his
voice. 'Home from university at last.' He put his hand
on her arm and drew her close to his side. 'Rose, meet
Stefanie.'

Rose's smile was warm as she regarded Stefanie and
her black eyes flashed with humour. 'The Stefanie Tom
and Aggie told me about, I think—not the one Jesse's
been talking about!'

Stefanie's stomach tightened at the reminder and she
grimaced. 'No—and that's something I'd better rectify
soon, before I chicken out and run into the washroom
to braid my hair!'

Rose laughed, although she seemed rather puzzled.
'Like Tom said, he'd be crazy not to prefer you like
this!'

Rose said that as though Jesse would care—but what
about Louisa? The questions pounded in her mind, the
memory of the two of them on the beach heartbreak-
ingly fresh. Before she could even think to ask them,
Jim was at her side and the opportunity was lost.

If Tom and Rose were surprised to see her with Jim,
they gave no sign and the four of them talked easily
until more guests arrived. Jim took her elbow and
guided her to a table on the edge of the dance floor,
before going for drinks.

Stefanie sat back and looked around. The hall was
filling rapidly and there were quite a mixture of
people—young, old and every age in between. In a
community this size everyone was a friend and
invitations were extended to all. Already there was an
element of cheer and excitement in the air, as though
everyone planned on having a good time. There was no
band, but one long-haired young man had set up his
stereo and was busy sorting through stacks of albums
and tapes.

In any other circumstances, Stefanie would have been
in the mood for dancing and just generally having a
good time. Tonight, however, she felt jumpy and

nervous, very conscious of the confrontation that loomed in the very near future. She stifled a sigh as Jim returned with her drink. She felt decidedly guilty for using him and was determined not to ruin his evening by being a gloomy partner. She sipped her drink, smiled at him over the rim of her glass and began to chat brightly.

Jim was entertaining and in any other circumstances she would have enjoyed his attention. His obvious admiration was flattering, certainly a boon to her ego. Besides, as a girl she had been caught up in the romanticism surrounding the red-coated Mounties, and while Jim was still too young and fresh-looking to fit the leading role, he was an interesting and intelligent man. While they sipped their drinks, he told her briefly about his boyhood in a small Saskatchewan town and his early desire to join the R.C.M.P.

'It was the uniform that did it,' he readily confessed. 'And the horses! It wasn't until I got older that I realised those were only for shows and special occasions.'

'But by then you were hooked,' Stefanie smiled with understanding. 'How long have you been stationed out here?'

'Two years—it's my second posting,' Jim explained. 'I like it, too. The people are friendly—and it's relatively peaceful, crime-wise!' he finished with a grin.

'So you've known Tom and—and everyone for a while now.'

Jim nodded. 'Tom has become a good friend—and Jess too, though I didn't see much of him until this fall.'

Just hearing Jesse's name was enough to make her heart skip a beat. Stefanie casually scanned the hall searching for him, knowing he would stand out to her like a light in the forest. He wasn't there. Forcing a smile, she turned her attention back to Jim.

'Enough about me,' he was saying. 'Tell me about yourself.' He propped his elbows on the table and leaned towards her, an expectant look on his face.

Stefanie had to laugh. 'You look like you're expecting quite a story. It isn't much!' She drew a deep breath and recited with a smile. 'I was born in Toronto, moved to Northern Manitoba when I was about five. I grew up in the bush and when I was fifteen got sent to Winnipeg for—for schooling. I took a commerce degree at the University of Manitoba and eventually worked as a chartered accountant. About a month ago I chucked the whole thing and moved out here to start again.' She leaned back in her chair and grinned. 'There—that's it!'

'In a nutshell,' Jim laughed, and looked at her with an element of respect. 'I'm impressed,' he admitted. 'All that beauty—and brains too! Who would have thought you'd be an accountant?'

Stefanie grinned and shrugged. 'Someone has to do it!'

He looked slightly puzzled. 'Does Jess know any of this? About you, I mean? It doesn't quite tie in with what he told me about you the other night. Not,' he hastened to add, 'that we were talking about you or anything. I was just—well, wondering who you were.' He flushed slightly.

'No—he doesn't,' Stefanie had to confess. 'I guess we never really talked about me.' Just some silly little girl who doesn't even exist! Because she knew she couldn't talk about Jesse without giving herself away, she turned the conversation to more general topics. She chatted easily, all the time making covert glances around the hall for Jesse. A mixture of anticipation and dread was making her more nervous by the minute. She finished her drink rather quickly and readily accepted Jim's offer of another, using his absence to try and spot Jesse.

It was Aggie she saw, and she knew that Jesse must have arrived as well. Quickly, before Jim returned, she made her way through the throng of people.

'Aggie!' she exclaimed, coming up to the old woman. 'How are you? You look great,' she added, admiring Aggie's lilac-coloured dress.

Aggie waved a deprecating hand. 'Me, I look okay. Now you—you look beautiful.'

'Why, thank you ma'am,' Stefanie said gaily. 'It was nice to have an excuse to dress up. I never thought I'd get sick of jeans!' She hesitated for a moment and then, deciding to adopt Aggie's forthright manner, asked directly, 'Where's Jesse?'

'Right behind you an' coming up fast,' was her instant reply. 'I think I go now, talk to Rosie's folks.' With a sly grin, Aggie deserted her. Drawing a deep if somewhat shaky breath, Stefanie erased the surprise from her face and turned around.

He was standing only a few feet away watching her intently as she turned. His eyes held hers and she stared back at him, her eyes wide and her lips slightly parted. My God, he's handsome, she thought, licking her lips nervously. He wore well cut grey slacks and a thin shirt of burgundy silk. Her heart thudded painfully at the flash she felt as his eyes blazed briefly into hers. And then the shutter dropped. He quickly closed the distance between them, a sardonic smile underlying the mocking grey eyes. Was it her he mocked?

'Well, well,' he drawled as his eyes roved slowly over her. 'Aren't we all dressed up tonight—such a pretty baby!'

Stefanie closed her eyes and willed for strength. 'Jesse . . .'

He held up a hand. 'I know, I know,' he said. 'You're not a baby.'

'No, I'm not,' said Stefanie, then continued deliberately, 'No more than I'm seventeen—and I'm not eighteen nor nineteen either!' There. It had been said.

Jesse's head came up and he stared at her hard, his face still and expressionless. 'How old?' he asked bluntly.

Stefanie swallowed hard. 'I—I'm twenty-six.' Her voice was weak and unsteady in spite of herself.

For a long moment there was silence. She stared at Jesse beseechingly, watching a mixture of expressions race through his eyes. Watched with a sinking heart as they darkened into a cold grey. Not knowing how to explain, she remained silent.

His eyes narrowed, the coldness slowly replaced by a smouldering anger. 'Just what the hell have you been playing at?' He ground out the words past clenched-teeth.

Stefanie winced. 'I'm sorry, Jesse,' she whispered. 'I never meant . . .'

'Just what did you mean?' he asked, a sneer curling his lip.

Stefanie drew back from the rage she sensed in him, knowing full well it was warranted. The deception had gone too far, long past the point where it could have been easily explained. She licked her lips nervously. 'I'm sorry, Jesse,' she said again, knowing the futility of her apology. 'I should have told you before, I know, but I just didn't know how to go about it. And Aggie thought . . .'

'Aggie!' he interrupted angrily. 'And Tom too, judging by some of the remarks he's made lately. Just what in hell were you trying to pull off?' His hands clenched tightly at his sides.

'Nothing!' Stefanie glared at him, feeling a sudden anger of her own. 'You're the one who started the damn thing in the first place by jumping to conclusions! Tom and Aggie just thought it was funny, that's all!'

'And what about you, Stefanie? Did you think it was funny? Is that how you get your kicks?' he taunted, reaching with barely controlled anger to grip her shoulders tightly.

Stefanie felt the anger flow through his hands into her, saw it in the stiff stance of his body, and heard it in the rasp of his voice. But behind the anger in his eyes she saw something else, an echo of the feelings that were causing her breath to quicken and her legs to tremble. She stared at him, her eyes wide and hiding nothing. Her lips parted softly. 'Jesse,' she whispered tentatively.

'Save it,' he said crudely, his hands dropping from her shoulders with startling suddenness. 'Your—date—is waiting.' He turned and walked away.

Sharp tears pricked her eyes as she watched him cross the hall. He moved quickly as though he couldn't get away from her fast enough. And then, knowing there was nothing she could do at the moment, she raised her head proudly and made her way back to Jim.

'What was that all about?' he asked as soon as she was seated.

'What?'

'That,' he said, pointing to where she had been standing. 'With Jess. I'd say he was plenty mad.'

'Not much,' she said, trying to sound casual. 'Just a—a little misunderstanding.'

'A pretty big one. I'd say,' Jim said dryly. 'I've never even seen Jess annoyed at anything before—and he was furious!'

Stefanie winced. 'Was it that obvious?'

He shook his head. 'I'm a trained investigator, remember. But the sparks were really flying out there for a while!' He looked closely at her, not missing the over-bright eyes or the tremble in her hands as she nervously tapped a nail on the side of her glass. 'What is it between you two, Stefanie?'

There was more than idle curiosity behind his question, and Stefanie liked him enough to want to be honest. 'I—it's a long story, Jim,' she said, 'but basically—well, Jesse had the wrong idea about my age and ...' How ridiculous it sounded! She gave an embarrassed shrug and stopped.

'Unless I miss my guess,' Jim said with a grin, 'the truth just came out!'

Stefanie nodded with a rueful grimace. 'The whole thing was so damned stupid!' She stared at her fingers. 'I don't know why I let it go so far. Of course he's angry—he's got every right to be!'

He reached across the table and loosened her fingers from their tight grip on the glass and held them gently in his big hands. 'You really like him, don't you, Stefanie?' he asked softly.

Stefanie nodded, blinking back quick tears. 'A lot,' she whispered. She looked at him, her eyes wide with misery. 'I'm sorry, Jim.'

'What for?' He smiled reassuringly. 'We can be friends, can't we?' He glanced over his shoulder and then leaned closer to say in a low tone, 'Don't look now, but we're being watched!'

Stefanie looked startled, caught the twinkle in Jim's eye and asked, 'Jesse?'

Jim nodded and said with a grin, 'And jealous as hell too, from the look on his face.'

She grimaced. 'That's called fury, Jim—not jealousy.'

He shook his head. 'It's more than that—I'm the one he's glaring at!' He turned in his chair until he was sitting even closer. 'Want to drive him crazy?'

She frowned. 'What do you mean?'

'Let's make him really jealous,' Jim explained. 'It'll take his mind off being angry.'

She looked doubtful and said with a sigh, 'I don't know, Jim. He'll probably just get madder—if that's possible!'

'At me, I'll bet, not you.' Jim squared his shoulders and said with a laugh, 'I can take it.'

'Why should you?'

'Let's just say I'd like to help smooth the rocky path of true love,' he drawled with a keen glance at the flush that stained her cheeks.

Love? Stefanie shook her head in surprise. She turned quickly and looked across the hall, catching Jesse's intense stare and holding it with a plea for understanding until he turned his back on her with a deliberate show of scorn. Love? The question quavered with white brightness in her mind and was answered with crystal-clear suddenness.

'You do love him, don't you?' Jim asked gently.

'Y—yes.' Stefanie managed a wan smile, then blurted dolefully, 'And he hates me!'

'Hardly!' Jim laughed. 'Cheer up, Stef. Let him think you're having a good time.'

She felt a flood of guilt. She was on a date with one man and mooning about another! 'I'm sorry, Jim, this isn't at all fair to you.'

'You don't owe me anything, Stef. And I must confess that there's someone back home I'm very close to—she's coming out this summer and, well . . .' Jim shrugged, 'like I said, we can be friends.'

'We are already,' Stefanie said warmly, feeling a quick and genuine affection grow for him.

'Okay, pal,' Jim grinned. 'Let's give that man over there a show that'll really make him turn green!' He stood up and held out his hand with a flourish, and they joined the growing group on the dance floor.

Jim was a surprisingly good dancer, moving to the music with a very real enthusiasm. Stefanie had a sneaking suspicion that he was secretly enjoying himself, although she was sure it was wasted on Jesse. Jim's right about one thing though, she thought. There's no reason for me to sit in a corner all night being miserable. Slowly, her spirits were lifting.

She knew suddenly that Jesse was watching, felt the burning heat of his stare that dropped unfailingly whenever she tried to catch it. Tossing her head defiantly, she joined in the dancing with an abandon she rarely showed in public, matching Jim's outrageous steps with more of her own. Others joined them and soon they were in the middle of a laughing group joined together by their uninhibited enjoyment of the music.

'It's working!' Jim whispered, holding her close for a moment. 'Keep it up—you look like you're having a ball!'

'I am,' Stefanie laughed. Her eyes glistened with emerald light and her hair flowed in fiery waves around her shoulders. It was hard to stay miserable surrounded by such merry people. She put her hands on Jim's shoulders, laughing up at him. 'Thanks, Jim.'

'Any time,' he said blithely, and whirled her around in his arms so fast she almost collided with another dancer.

It was Jesse. His face was impassive under the cover of his glossy beard, but the eyes that held hers were burning with fury. Stefanie cringed as his expression changed and she saw furrows of contempt etched deep on his brow, then he danced away. She stumbled and clutched Jim tightly, all her hard-won pleasure gone.

'I—let's sit down, Jim,' she whispered. Quickly she walked to their table, followed closely by a sympathetic Jim.

'Want a refill?' he asked, indicating her empty glass.

'Please.' Stefanie nodded as she sat down, and turned to watch the dancers with a fixed smile as Jim made his way to the bar. She watched Jesse whenever she could. She could feel his anger in every cell of her body and knew he wasn't going to forgive her deceit easily. Her smile slipped and she gave a rather woebegone sigh.

'It's that bad, is it?'

Startled, she looked up into Rose's questioning eyes. Knowing exactly what she meant, Stefanie nodded. 'He's furious—and the worst thing is, he's got every right to be!'

Rose dropped into Jim's vacated chair and studied her closely. 'I don't know what's going on between you two, Stefanie, and to be honest, if Aggie didn't have such a high opinion of you . . .'

Stefanie winced at the censure she heard in Rose's voice. 'I've really made a mess of things,' she admitted, embarrassed.

'How is Jim involved in all this?' Rose asked bluntly.

'He's my friend,' Stefanie said simply.

Rose accepted the simple statement with a nod. 'I suppose it isn't any of my business, but Jesse has been my friend—a very close friend—for most of my life. He was hurt badly once, and I don't want to see it happen again.'

Hurt? The word was unexpected and Stefanie looked at Rose with questioning eyes.

'If he can be that angry with you, he can be hurt by you.' Rose's voice was softened by what she saw in Stefanie's clear eyes. 'Why did you lie to him like that?' she asked, her curiosity gentle.

'I didn't exactly lie,' Stefanie explained miserably, her fingers beating a nervous tattoo on the table. 'At least, not at first. Jesse just assumed I was younger than I am. A lot younger,' she added with a grimace. 'I didn't set him straight when I should have, and the whole thing just—just snowballed!'

Rose shook her cap of shining black hair and looked at Stefanie shrewdly, a glimmer of understanding beginning to grow in her dark eyes. 'What are you going to do about it?'

'Just hope he'll cool down enough to let me explain.'

'Can you?'

'I'll have to try.' Stefanie's voice was quietly determined.

'Well,' said Rose, her voice friendlier, 'don't brood about it too much. Jesse doesn't hold a grudge for long.' She leaned closer, her eyes bright with laughter. 'If it'll make you feel any better,' she whispered, 'I'd say it was Jim he had it in for! You two really know how to cut up on the dance floor,' she giggled, 'and if looks could kill, we'd be carrying poor Jim out on a stretcher!'

'That—that was Jim's intention,' Stefanie confessed, and received an understanding smile. How nice Jesse's friends were—and how astute! The air was cleared and she and Rose began to talk easily.

He was there, standing with startling suddenness beside her chair. Strong fingers gripped her wrist and, with obvious reluctance, Stefanie forced her eyes over his tautly held hips, over the thin burgundy silk straining to cover his wide shoulders; dragged her eyes past the glossy black beard and met his smouldering stare. Unable to hold his look, she dropped her gaze quickly, staring at the table.

'Excuse us, Rose.' The words were tight. 'Stefanie owes me a dance.' His fingers tightened painfully and he pulled her to her feet.

Stefanie followed him reluctantly on to the dance floor, her pleading look back at Rose met with an amused shrug. Jesse stopped abruptly in the middle of the dimly lit hall, his fingers bruising her wrist as he pulled her closer.

'You're hurting me,' Stefanie muttered.

'Good,' he said succinctly, his eyes sweeping from her face to follow the creamy rise of her throat down to linger on the tantalising peep of black lace covering the snowy swell of her breasts. With an unintelligible mutter, he pulled her tight against him.

Stefanie brought her hands up to push against him, trying to maintain a saving distance from his heady closeness. It was useless. Her hands splayed helplessly on the heat of his chest, absorbing the intoxicating beat of his heart. She fought hard to prevent her will-less

body from pressing closer to his litheness and stared
woodenly over his shoulder as he took up the slow
rhythm of the dance. She held herself stiffly against the
rush of desire that threatened to weaken her until she
would have no choice but to lean against him.

'Relax,' he whispered, slipping his hands from her
shoulders to run them lightly down her back until they
came to rest on her waist, his thumbs sensually stroking
her hips.

Stefanie had no control over the shudder of desire
that shot through her at his touch and knew from the
convulsive clutch of his fingers that he had felt it too.
Her eyes flew to his face to find he was watching her
closely. Mesmerised by what she saw in his eyes, she
offered no resistance as he drew her nearer. Her arms
moved from his chest to rest lightly on his shoulders
and then slowly crept up to clasp around his neck. Her
breasts tingled as they pushed against his chest and
ripples of desire burned through her, leaving her pliant
to the hypnotising rhythm of his body.

It was too much. Biting back a moan, Stefanie buried
her face in his shoulder, risking the closer contact lest
he should see what must be blatantly obvious in her
eyes; see her utter helplessness in the torrent of desire
his touch aroused.

'What are you?' he whispered harshly. 'Pretty child or
beautiful woman?' His fingers raked through the flame
of her hair. 'Do I know you at all?'

Stefanie raised her head and smiled tremulously at
him. 'You know me,' she whispered. She felt his swift
intake of breath, saw the grey eyes narrow as they
probed hers, saw them start to soften with the glimmer
of a smile. Then the music ended.

Jesse slowed to a stop still holding her against him.
Suddenly selfconscious, Stefanie loosened her hold on
his neck and pushed at him until there was a more
respectable distance between them. Once again she
avoided his eyes, horribly aware that she had given
away too much, seduced by the music and his nearness.

'I—I should go sit down,' she said breathlessly,
staring at his chest. 'Jim . . .'

Jesse's hands fell away quickly and his lips tightened. 'Yes,' he said curtly. 'Jim.' His grip was tight as he led her back to her table.

Jim's face was grave and he came forward as soon as he saw them. 'Stefanie,' he began without preamble, 'there's been a bad accident on the highway—I've got to go.' His face was grim at the thought of the carnage waiting for him. 'Sorry.'

Stefanie touched his arm sympathetically. 'Don't worry about me Jim—go.' She smiled warmly. 'Thank you, Jim—it's been fun.'

'It has, hasn't it?' His grin was brief. He glanced quickly at Jesse. 'Let's finish it some other evening, shall we?' he asked with a wink. 'Say Monday night?'

'I—okay, Jim.' Stefanie managed a smile, then winced as Jesse's hand tightened painfully on her arm.

Jim grabbed his jacket, calling over his shoulder as he walked away, 'Oh, Jess, do me a favour, will you? Give Stef a ride home—you're going in that direction anyway.' The grin he gave Stefanie was positively wicked as he waved and walked away.

Stefanie groaned inwardly. In spite of his good intentions, Jim had made things worse. She sat down quickly, aware of Jesse's stony silence. 'It's okay,' she said, nervously sipping her drink. 'I'll find another ride.'

'Like hell you will!' he muttered forcefully. 'I'll take you. But first,' he added, coming up behind her chair, his fingers biting into her shoulders, 'we're going to dance.' His voice was low and threatening. 'Come on.'

Not daring—not wanting—to refuse him, Stefanie took a fortifying gulp of her drink and followed him on to the dance floor.

'Jesse,' she pleaded as he turned impassively and held out his arms, 'I—I'd rather just go straight home.' Standing so close, she was terribly aware of his distance.

'Not yet,' he said shortly, and then, softly, with a hint of a plea in his voice, 'Dance with me, Stefanie.'

Unable to resist, Stefanie moved quickly into his arms, trying vainly to suppress the shivers of desire the mere anticipation of his touch aroused. Sighing in resignation, she laid her head on his shoulder as he folded her into his arms. How long she had waited for passion's touch. How helpless she was in its wake! Accepting what she had no will to control, she melted against him, her lithe body soft against his tantalising hardness. She heard a rumble of sound from deep in his chest as his arms tightened around her and his cheek came to rest on her head, his warm breath stirring the shimmering embers of her hair. Their steps slowed until the dance was little more than a timeless embrace in the dimness of the hall.

'Stefanie,' he murmured.

'Hmm?'

'Let's go,' he said, pushing her back slightly until she raised her head.

'Why?' she asked, blinking emerald bright eyes.

He nuzzled his reply against the soft skin of her cheek. 'I want to kiss you.'

The words were spoken with such an intensity that her breath caught sharply. She stared at him, her eyes glazing with an excitement she couldn't suppress. 'Yes,' she whispered huskily. 'Oh yes!'

Jesse's eyes narrowed with ardour and without another word he took her hand in a heated clasp and led her away. No words were spoken as he helped her into her coat, but his fingers lingered as he buttoned it for her, his eyes fixed on her trembling lips.

The spell of desire stayed with them in the quiet darkness of the ride to her place. Jesse took the key from her shaking fingers, pushed the door open impatiently and turned to her, his eyes brilliant with an exigency she wanted desperately to answer. Could she? In the harsh light of the kitchen, anxiety grew. Nervously nibbling her bottom lip, Stefanie slipped out of her coat.

'I—I'll make some coffee,' she stalled.

'Forget the coffee,' he said in low vibrant tones. 'Come here.'

'I—I'd like some,' she persisted, her eyes unconsciously pleading. 'Maybe you could—could light the fire.'

Jesse looked at her closely, his eyes narrow with

speculation, then he nodded briefly and turned to do
her bidding. 'Don't be long,' he warned.

Stefanie leaned weakly against the counter top
waiting for the coffee to brew, fighting the persistent
flutter of fear that threatened her. She wanted
desperately to run into Jesse's arms demanding his
kisses and caresses, but ... Tell him! a tiny voice
cautioned. He'll listen! Stefanie shook her head and
placed mugs on the tray with the coffee, stilling the
warning whispers. She picked up the tray and went into
the living room. I want him! she thought determinedly.

He was standing in front of the blazing fire, hands
thrust into his pockets so that the material of his slacks
stretched tautly over his thighs. Stefanie swallowed
convulsively at the sight of him. Oh, God, how I want
him! she cried silently, and trembled anew at the sweet
flood of desire he so easily aroused. He came forward
quickly, plucked the tray from her unresisting fingers
and set it on the hearth.

He straightened up slowly and turned to look at her,
capturing her wide green eyes in a smouldering stare.
'Stefanie,' he whispered hoarsely, and with a sharp cry
she flung herself into his arms, raising her face blindly
for his kiss.

The crush of his lips fanned the fire in her into an
inferno. With a whimper she pressed against his
hardness, parting her lips at his insistence. She drank
deeply of the sweetness of his mouth, her arms
wrapping around his neck holding tight as the fever of
desire trembled in her legs, stunned beyond reason at
the power of his kiss.

'God, Stefanie,' he groaned against her quivering lips,
'I've wanted to do that for a long time. One hell of a
long time,' he muttered, and claimed her lips again.

His hands moved over her throbbing body, pressing
her hips even closer to his arousal. His mouth
demanded, and received, passion from the very core of
her being. Tearing his lips away, he kissed with moist
heat over her cheeks, touched her soft throat with fire,
seeking the satiny swell of her breasts, already taut and
pulsating in anticipation of his touch.

With a groan of impatience his hands slid under the concealing material of her jumpsuit, tugging at the material until it slid down. Her bare shoulders glowed pearl-white in the flickering firelight, and her breasts were a tantalising gleam under the delicate black lace of her camisole.

'Beautiful,' he breathed. His trembling fingers traced the gold chain that shone between her breasts, moving down with an aching slowness to stroke her hardening nipples through the silky material. Stefanie moaned with growing fervour, raking her fingers through his hair as he slowly lowered his head to kiss each thrusting peak through its lacy cover.

With a sudden sound of impatience, Jesse brushed the tiny straps from her shoulders and watched with passion-filled eyes as the lace slid down slowly, catching for an instant on her roseate nipples before falling around her waist. He sat back, staring at her beauty.

'Touch me, Stefanie,' he demanded hoarsely. 'Show me how much you want me—show me what you can do.'

Do? Stefanie swallowed uneasily and licked her passion-stung lips. Unsure, she stared at him, the doubts of many years stirring restlessly.

Misreading her hesitation, Jesse grabbed her bare shoulders. 'Don't tease,' he begged, his voice thick and raspy. 'You've stopped playing a little girl—show me what a woman you are!'

His words, intended to challenge a woman of experience, withered Stefanie's new-found confidence, and once again she doubted her sexuality. Fearing she couldn't give him what he wanted, she shrank from him. Tell him! her senses screamed with frustrated arousal, but already it was too late. She saw his eyes narrow and darken, a look of total disbelief preceeding the anger.

Gulping with trepidation, she shook off his hold, sliding her arms back into the scant cover of her camisole. 'Jesse, I—I'm sorry . . .' The words stuck in her throat. 'I—I can't!' she burst out with difficulty.

'Can't?' he said with growing rage. 'Won't! You little

. . .' he bit the word off savagely. 'What crazy game are you playing this time?' he seethed. 'Those were no innocent little goodnight kisses you were handing out there—you knew damned well where they were going!' He had crossed the line from intense arousal to black anger and reached for her with menace, scowling darkly as she scrambled out of reach.

'Forget the scandalised virgin act, Stefanie,' he jeered, grabbing her arm with biting fingers to pull her close. 'It's too late.' His voice thickened as he ran his fingers under the straps of her camisole with a touch that had lost all gentleness.

The resonant clang of his angry words pierced wounds only recently begun to heal. Filled with pain and growing terror, Stefanie pushed hard against his chest, desperately fighting the passions she had so willingly aroused in him.

'Is it the fight you like?' he whispered hoarsely, his teeth nipping against her tender skin. 'Is that what turns you on?'

'No! Oh God, no!' The words tore from her throat in an agonised cry. She beat at the solid wall of his chest, felt the material tear free from his clenching hands and fled for the stairs, her hands cupped over ashen lips, leaving Jesse stunned with dawning awareness.

She slammed the bathroom door behind her, locking it with shaking fingers. Nausea washed over her in chilling waves and she leaned against the sink heaving with a sickness that went far beyond the physical.

'Stefanie?' Jesse's voice came, low with anxiety from behind the locked door. 'Are you all right?'

She heard the words but not the concern. 'Go away,' she sobbed. 'Just—go!'

'Not until I know you're okay,' he insisted, and then his voice softened in plea. 'Please, Stefanie, open the door!'

'Why?' she croaked. 'So you can h-hit me? Or rape me, like—like . . .' She stopped with a tortured moan of humiliation. 'Leave me alone!' Her voice rose hysterically.

'Not yet,' he said though the door. 'I promise—I

won't hurt you. I just want to make sure you're all right.'

'All right!' she repeated wildly. 'I'll never be all right!' Her last vestige of control cracked and she turned to pound with sobbing fury on the door that separated them. 'Go home, Jesse,' she cried. 'Go . . . home!'

Jesse closed his eyes at the torment in her voice, sickened with himself. He rubbed his forehead in agitation and let out a deep breath. 'Okay, Stefanie,' he said with forced calm, 'I'll go. We'll talk tomorrow.' He didn't leave. He stood in the darkness of the stairway, hands clenched into tight fists as he silently cursed his brute insensitivity. It seemed an eternity before the door opened.

Stefanie stumbled across the room, exhausted by the emotions that had torn through her. With a shaky sigh that touched the hidden man's heart, she dropped on to the bed, clutching a pillow tightly against her chest.

Jesse came towards her with hesitant steps. 'Stefanie?' His voice was soft and filled with concern.

She was too drained to feel surprise. 'I thought you were gone,' she said dully.

'I couldn't go until I knew you were okay,' he said, kneeling beside the bed. He touched her shoulder tentatively, withdrawing his hand quickly at her restless move.

'Go home, Jesse.' Her voice was flat with a deep weariness and she stared blankly into the dark corners of the room.

He hesitated briefly, then with a slight sigh, stood up. 'I'll go,' he said. 'And Stefanie—for what it's worth, I'm sorry. Very sorry.' He took the comforter from the foot of the bed and drew it over her. With a bleak look at her unresponsive figure, he slipped silently away.

CHAPTER SEVEN

STEFANIE slept long and heavily. When finally she could use sleep as an escape no longer, she rose and dressed quickly in jeans and a sweater. She ran downstairs, eyes carefully averted to avoid seeing the unused coffee cups in front of the cold ashes in the fireplace. Then, grabbing her jacket, she left the house for the beach.

The sullen greyness of the day suited her mood perfectly, and she walked slowly, still numb, still on the edge of despair, ravaged by the tumult of last night's fiasco. Feeling drained of energy, she climbed a rugged black rock and found a niche where she could sit and watch the rolling ocean.

She loved Jesse, loved the big gentle man who had been her friend, but last night he had been a stranger. She shuddered at the memory of his cold withdrawn face when he had learned her true age. She remembered his fury when fear had overcome her passion, and knew that with her instant and passionate response to his kisses, she had unwittingly deceived him a second time. She should have told him.

What a mess she had made of things! She hugged her knees to her chest. And I thought I was playing it safe! she thought bitterly. Tears stung her eyes and she buried her head in her arms, struggling to retain her fragile grip on sanity.

'Stefanie . . .'

Her head flew up and she stared with eyes wide in her pale face. 'J-Jesse,' she whispered, then pain crossed her face and she turned away. 'Leave me alone.' Her voice was harsh.

'No,' he said firmly, dropping his long length on to the rock beside her. He looked at her impassive face as she stared deliberately over the water. Hesitatingly, he reached out to touch her arm, but his fingers clenched and withdrew before he could make contact. 'Stefanie, we've got to talk.'

Stefanie sat in stony silence.

Jesse sighed, raking his fingers through his hair. 'Last night . . .'

'I don't want to talk about it!' The words burst past her tight lips and she clambered up, desperate to leave.

'Stay!' he commanded, pulling her back down beside him, his hand firm on her arm. 'Please stay,' he repeated softly, his hand gentle now. Stefanie stayed, but refused to look at him.

Jesse let out a slow breath. 'I was a—a brute last night. I'm sorry—damned sorry.' Still she stared out over the water.

'Stefanie,' he pleaded, 'look at me.' His hand cupped her chin and he turned her face until she had no choice but to look at him, her eyes wide and vulnerable in a frame of wind-tangled hair. His thumb stroked her cheek and his eyes held hers with compassion in their depths. 'I hurt you last night, and I'm sorry. I shouldn't have assumed that because you were older you were . . . willing.'

Stefanie winced and pulled away from him. She had been willing last night, instinctively passionate and desiring. What should have been a beautiful and sharing time had been shattered because of her ignorance. 'It wasn't just y-you,' she whispered unsteadily. 'S-something happened a long t-time ago. I should have told . . .' Helplessly she stopped. How could she begin to recount the emotional devastation that had been the basis of her reaction last night? Biting her lip, she mumbled, 'I'm sorry.'

'Don't!' he said roughly. 'You have nothing to apologise for.' His hands came up around her shoulders and he pulled her into his arms. One hand came up to smooth her tangled hair and with a shuddering sigh she burrowed her face into the warmth of his neck, absorbing the steady rhythm of his thudding heart, the gentle strength of his embrace. This was the man she loved.

'Friends?' he murmured into the auburn tumble of hair.

'Friends,' she agreed softly, clinging to his warmth, feeling hope stir again. Suddenly the world seemed a bright and beautiful place. She raised her head, her eyes alight with emerald brilliance. She leaned back in the circle of his arms and smiled at him. 'I'm starving!'

Jesse's eyes crinkled and he gave a shout of the laughter she so loved to hear. 'So let's go eat!'

They walked along the beach, Jesse's arm slung companionably over her shoulders, and Stefanie, happy with the closeness, slid her arm around his waist.

'My place or yours?' he asked.

'Yours—that is, can you cook?'

'If I say I'm a lousy cook, will you do it?'

'I'll risk it,' she said, laughing up at him. 'I'm hungry enough to eat anything.'

'Ah well,' he sighed. 'It would have been a lie anyway—I'm a great cook!'

He was. They ate the crisp bacon and creamy scrambled eggs with enjoyment, finishing off with toast spread thick with delicious blackberry jam.

'This jam is fantastic,' Stefanie said as she popped the last crust into her mouth. 'Who made it?'

'I did,' Jesse said smugly. 'And I must say my blackberry pie is even better.'

'Well,' she commented with amusement, 'there's certainly a lot more to you than meets the eye!'

'As with you, Stefanie.' He was smiling, but there was a hint of seriousness in his eyes. 'In fact, I find I know very little about you. Tell me.'

Stefanie hesitated. What was it he wanted to know?

'Just the bare facts, Stefanie,' he said, reading her hesitation. 'For now. The rest will wait.'

That she could handle. The rest—the deep wounds and emotional scars—that would have to wait for another time. Sipping her coffee, she went lightly over the details of her life.

Jesse leaned back in his chair, laughter lurking in his eyes. 'Who would have thought it—a twenty-six-year-old accountant wandering around the beach with braids and those ridiculous overalls! You didn't look a day over eighteen.' He shook his head ruefully.

'You—you never suspected?'

'Well,' he drawled lazily, 'I did think you were unusually mature for your age. Precocious, I think I called it.' He chuckled at the sweep of colour in her cheeks.

'I was awful, wasn't I?'

'A brat,' he agreed readily. He smiled, and his eyes were warm, but he continued to regard her with a peculiar intensity. Disconcerted, Stefanie got up quickly and began to clear the table, neatly stacking the dishes beside the sink. Was he going to ask about last night's obvious terror? His next questions, however, were reassuringly innocuous, and Stefanie happily filled him in on her move, her new job and her plans to find a place to live in Vancouver.

'I'd love to live near English Bay,' she confessed as she dried the dishes he washed. 'I'd love to be near the water and Stanley Park.'

'An apartment in that area will be expensive,' he warned, giving the counter top a wipe.

She raised an eyebrow. 'I'm sure my salary is more than adequate,' she said somewhat haughtily as she neatly folded her tea towel.

'Ah, yes—you're not just a fledgling file clerk. I was forgetting.' He leaned back against the counter. 'It's those eyes,' he said softly, his hand coming up quickly to capture her chin, forcing her to look directly at him. 'They're just too damned innocent to belong to a twenty-six-year-old woman.' He smiled gently as she lowered her eyes in sudden confusion, rubbing his thumb against the warm rush of colour on her fair skin. 'Just how innocent are you, Stefanie?'

Stefanie willed her voice to be steady. 'That's for me to know and you to find out,' she whispered coyly, and reached up to flutter her lips across his. On his sharp intake of breath, she slipped from his grasp, grabbed her jacket and with a quick wave of her fingers, left.

Hot steamy baths were definitely no longer relaxing.

Stefanie had drawn a tubful of water shortly after she arrived home, but as soon as she slid under the perfumed water, the intoxicating visions started.

She could see Jesse as he had been the night she had run to him in terror. She remembered how the water from his shower clung to his muscled chest and to the dark sprinkle of hair that curled down from his flat stomach until it was hidden by the skimpy towel that her errant fingers had longed to throw aside. And she remembered his touches of last night; remembered the searing kisses and the incredibly erotic touch of his lips on her breasts; remembered the fire in her loins as he pulled her tight against the hardness of his hips . . .

Stefanie groaned loudly in pure frustration. She climbed quickly out of the tub and towelled herself dry with unusual force. Innocent! she chortled to herself. Her eyes obviously didn't mirror her thoughts! Belting a robe around her slim waist, she went downstairs.

Much later she sat by the fire listening to music, a reflective light in her green eyes. She could not deny that she wanted Jesse with both a physical and emotional need almost overwhelming in intensity. But . . . how did Jesse feel about her? He liked her, yes— maybe even wanted her . . . but was there any more?

Could she let him make love to her knowing that there would be no declarations of undying love, no promises to live happily ever after? And what about afterwards, when he was satiated with her, wanting nothing more than a friendly parting of the ways— could she bear it? Stefanie shuddered violently, already knowing the pain that separation would cause.

She had two choices. She could leave now while she was still relatively intact, or . . . she stood up abruptly and went to stand by the window, staring out into the darkness. Who was she trying to fool? She was not intact—Jesse held her heart whether he wanted it or not. The decision had been made long ago. She would take whatever he could give her for as long as he wanted her. She had no choice.

Resolutely she climbed the stairs to her bed and slid under the covers. She closed her eyes, determinedly pushing away the disturbing picture of Louisa as she stood yawning with ripe sexuality in Jesse's doorway. She had no choice. She would have to trust him.

He stood silently in the pre-dawn greyness of her room, staring with a bemused smile at the bewitching picture of innocence. Her hair splashed in wine-dark waves over the pillow's whiteness, a slender hand curled under the soft curve of her cheek. The cat, tucked firmly in the hook of her knees, glowered at him with shining yellow orbs as he crossed the floor and knelt beside the bed.

'Stefanie.'

The soft sibilant sound stirred her sleep. Her eyes flickered open and she looked at him without surprise. 'Hello, dream,' she whispered, reaching up to run her hand over the crispness of his beard.

'Hello, witch,' he answered. He turned his head to touch his lips to her palm, hiding a smile as her eyes widened with dawning awareness and she withdrew her palm quickly.

'How—how did you get in?' she asked, somnolence fleeing.

'Your door was unlocked—what else?' he murmured, tracing a line from her brow to the tip of her nose. 'Did you know you have six freckles on your nose?'

'Seven,' she corrected, then frowned slightly. 'I don't like people watching me while I sleep!'

'Why not?' Jesse laughed softly. 'You do it very prettily. You don't snore, or drool, and your mouth doesn't hang open. Just enough,' he added leaning forward, 'to be . . . enticing.' His lips brushed hers with a kiss so sweet its brevity was torment.

'Jesse,' she murmured, wrapping her arms around his neck before he could pull away, inhaling deeply his warm man scent.

'Do you always sleep in the nude?' He nuzzled against the soft skin of her shoulder.

'Usually,' she admitted softly, running a hand through his hair, tousling the gold-tipped curls. She arched against his closeness as the moist heat of his mouth moved down to cover the soft swell of her hidden breasts. Then her moan turned into a gasp of surprise as he abruptly tore himself from her and stood up.

'Jesse?' Her voice was softly pleading.

'Get up, Stefanie,' he said, trying to steady his uneven breathing. 'Time to go.'

'Go? Go where?' She struggled to sit up, holding the covers closely over her bareness. There was a catch of surprise in her voice and her eyes were round with bewilderment.

'Out in the boat,' he said shortly, staring from under hooded eyes, unable to look away. Dawn was lightening the room, touching fiery fingers to the cascade of hair covering her gleaming shoulders. Abruptly he turned and grabbed her robe from the closet. 'Get dressed,' he said brusquely, throwing it on the bed.

'Who died and made you king?' she muttered crossly, stung by his about-face.

'Sorry.' His smile was brief. 'I meant to ask you yesterday if you would like to come out with me today, but you—er—left rather suddenly.'

Stefanie looked down quickly as she remembered the words and action preceding her hasty departure.

'Please come,' he cajoled softly. 'You'll enjoy it out on the water.'

'Oh—all right,' she said rather petulantly. 'Go make some coffee while I get dressed. Lots,' she added with a yawn, pushing the heavy fall of hair back from her face.

'Yes, Your Majesty,' he mocked with a smile, and with a last look, went down the narrow flight of stairs.

Stefanie lay back down as soon as he left, puzzling over his manner. He had awakened her in a way that was so sensuous she could have purred, but as soon as she had made a move to respond, he had pulled away. She sat back up, frowning. Could it be that, after all her soul-searching last night, he didn't want her? She had accepted that he didn't love her, but ... Stefanie grimaced and then shrugged. Hadn't she decided to take whatever he had to give her? And if that was nothing more than friendship, then so be it. Inwardly her heart raged in protest. It would never be enough.

'Hey, Stefanie—you up yet?' Jesse's voice cut through her thoughts. 'Better hurry!'

'Okay,' she called back quickly, not wanting him to come up to check. 'I'm up!'

She washed sketchily and drew on a pair of jeans and a T-shirt, adding a thick sweater for warmth. She ran a brush over her hair and tied it back with a filmy green scarf, and then, feeling somewhat shy, she went downstairs.

Jesse was standing by the stove, casual and handsome in a cream-coloured sweater and the inevitable faded jeans. Snug in all the right places, she thought, staring at him with a hunger that threatened the rigidity of her knees.

'Hungry?' asked Jesse, seeing her.

'What? Oh—yes,' she managed, dragging her eyes to his face. 'Starved!' She had to smile.

'I've made toast,' he said, and waved her to the table. 'Eat up, and we'll be off.'

'Where are we going?'

'You'll see,' he answered briefly as he joined her at the table, and she had to content herself with that.

'Is the boat in Tofino?' Stafanie asked later as she settled in his truck for the ride.

Jesse nodded. 'At the government dock.' He peered through the windshield at the cloudy sky. 'I was a bit concerned about the weather, but the marine forecast calls for a calm day.'

'Good,' said Stefanie, then confessed, 'I'm going to feel nervous enough out there.'

He laughed. 'Have no fear—no harm will befall you when you're with me!'

'That's reassuring,' she said dryly, clutching the dash tightly as he swerved sharply to avoid a pothole on the side of the road.

She looked down at the aluminium boat bobbing gently in the oily swell beside the wharf. 'That's it?' she asked doubtfully. 'It looks awfully small.'

'Only because it's tied up next to the bigger boats,' he explained. 'Get in.'

'I don't know,' Stefanie hesitated. 'I mean, if it looks this small here—what's it going to look like in the middle of all that?' She waved her hand towards the water. 'Infinitesimal!'

Jesse laughed. 'We won't go anywhere near the middle—I promise. Come on, Stef,' he coaxed. 'Don't you trust me?'

She wrinkled her nose at him. 'Well, since you put it like that . . . Do I at least get a lifejacket?'

'Certainly.' He reached under the seat and presented one to her, helping her to tie it securely. He offered his hand to assist her into the boat. 'Your carriage awaits, m'lady.'

Once they were under way, Stefanie began to relax. She trusted Jesse's common sense and knew he was competent on the water. She looked at him as he sat in the stern, one hand on the tiller of the small outboard. His bearded chin was thrust forward, his eyes far-seeing. He had a wool cap jammed on his curls and his jeans were tucked into high rubber boots. He was at home on the sea.

Stefanie relaxed completely. She was in good hands. She shifted in her seat until she could look over the bow as the little boat thrust its way through the green water, making a straight and steady line towards a distant point of land.

True to his word, Jesse kept the boat close to shore. Steep hills rolled from the distant cloud-wrapped mountains and dropped tree-covered sides straight into the water. There was no gradual slope ending in a sandy beach here, just a short sharp drop into the ocean.

'We're heading around that point!' Jesse shouted, waving an arm in the general direction.

Stefanie merely nodded, not wanting to talk over the noise of the engine. Braver now, she leaned closer to the side of the boat and peered into the water, but there was little visible beneath the surface. Except for a few pieces of driftwood and the occasional clump of seaweed, the ocean gave an illusion of bareness. The deep water didn't offer to view its teeming life.

Stefanie straightened up and looked out over the water. They approached the point with surprising speed and soon rounded it. She was beginning to wonder just where it was they were going, but the engine's loud throb kept her from asking. She contented herself with looking around, enjoying the damp and salty spray that misted her face. Time and time again she found her eyes slipping from the ocean view to seek Jesse's face. Her eyes raked over the strong profile, and she hugged the love she felt for him close to her heart.

Suddenly his expression changed. His eyes narrowed and he sat taller, staring intently ahead. His hand moved on the tiller and the motor cut to an idle hum. Stefanie felt her pulses quicken. What was it? She turned to stare in the same direction, squinting as she strained to see.

'See it?' he asked.

She shook her head. 'Nothing.'

'Keep watching,' he said as he took his camera from its pack.

'What am I watching for?'

'Whales,' he said briefly.

'W-whales?'

'Killer whales. Keep watching. They should surface any minute now.'

'Killer whales!' Stefanie moaned. 'Great—here we are floating about in this dinky little boat with killer whales swimming all around!'

Jesse chuckled. 'Don't panic. There isn't one recorded incident of a killer whale attacking humans.'

'Probably because no one ever lived to make a report,' she said sarcastically.

He laughed outright. 'Scared?'

'Who—me? Oh no, not at all.'

'Then relax and keep watching. It's a fascinating sight.'

Even as his words ended, the whales surfaced. Two huge creatures, their distinctive black and white bodies glistening, rose in perfect unison. Stefanie's breath caught in her throat in a mixture of fear and surprise and she clutched at the seat beneath her.

'What luck!' Jesse exclaimed. 'They're staying on the surface.'

'At least that way we won't have to worry about them coming up underneath the boat,' Stefanie said with relief, thinking again of the smallness of their craft.

'No worry,' he reassured her with a smile. 'They aren't travelling in this direction, and even if they were they'd leave us alone.'

She tried to relax. Jesse was obviously not bothered. If anything, he was rejoicing, busily taking pictures through his telescopic lens. The whales kept a good distance from the boat, and Stefanie watched with growing delight as they splashed and gambolled about—if such a huge creature can be said to gambol, Stefanie thought with a smile.

As she watched, the largest of the two disappeared from sight and reappeared suddenly, travelling upward so fast it shot right into the air. It seemed to hang there for a moment, a sharp silhouette against the grey sky, before falling back into the water with a resounding splash.

Stefanie clutched the side of the boat as it rocked in the shock waves of that last majestic display. 'Fantastic!' she breathed as the whales disappeared from sight.

'I knew you'd like it,' Jesse said with satisfaction as though he had arranged the whole thing for her benefit. He tucked his camera back in the pack, sped the engine up, and they were off over the waves at their original speed.

Gradually they made their way down the inlet, leaving the open ocean farther behind. Stefanie was totally relaxed now, trusting Jesse's seafaring instincts. She watched with no fear as he guided the boat slowly and surely through a narrow gap between two huge rocks.

'This is only passable when the tide is in,' he explained, 'and as it's just coming in now, we'll have plenty of time to get back before the water is too low.'

'Good,' she said. 'I'm not ready for a night on the beach just yet!' Warm as she was bundled up in her parka, there was a damp chill in the air. Winter wasn't ready to let go.

As the boat rounded the jutting rock, Stefanie knew what they had come to see. Rising high on the tiny beach in front of them were three splendidly carved totem poles, the silver-grey of the weathered cedar a stark contrast against a backdrop of forest green. Jesse cut the engine and they bobbed on the quiet water of the cove, absorbing the stately heritage of the West Coast Indians.

'Are they very old?' Stefanie asked after a quiet moment.

'Around a century,' Jesse answered. 'No one really knows for sure, nor why they're here. Some people think it's the sight of a great potlatch.'

'Potlatch?' The word was new to Stefanie.

'Yes—it's from a Nootka word meaning to give, a tradition among the Indians of the Pacific Northwest,' Jesse explained to her as he changed the lens on his camera. 'It was a gathering of people to witness an important event—a young person assuming an adult name, the completion of a house, things like that. The host would give away almost everything—things he had often worked years to acquire. The more he gave away—or, in some cases, destroyed—the more prestige he and his clan would have.'

'But he wouldn't have anything left,' Stefanie objected. 'It doesn't make sense.'

He shrugged, snapping a wide-angle lens into place. 'It was an effective means of distribution—and you could always count on getting back more than you gave at someone else's potlatch. The guests would consider it a matter of pride to try and outdo the host. It worked effectively until the tribes were inundated with white man's trade goods.'

As they drifted in, he took several pictures. Finally satisfied, he replaced his camera and started the engine just enough to push them to the sandy beach of the tiny cove. Stefanie jumped out as soon as the boat touched the shore and with a deft tug on the rope, pulled the bow on to the sand. She was standing at the base of the tallest totem pole examining the highly stylised carving when Jesse came to stand beside her.

'Magnificent, aren't they?' he asked softly, putting his hands on her shoulders. Even through the thickness of her parka, Stefanie was aware of his touch. Very aware. She rested against him and managed to nod in agreement.

'They tell stories,' he said, his cheek touching the side of her head. 'Family histories, legends—things like that. The animal carved on top usually represented the clan involved in the carving. Unfortunately,' he added with regret, 'there aren't all that many people left who can interpret them. But people like Aggie, with her stories, and Rose, with her art, are doing their best to see that the remaining knowledge is passed on.'

'Isn't that what your book does?' It was an effort to speak evenly. She was too aware of his hands on her shoulders, of the rub of his beard on her temple. Even his shrug added to her awareness.

'In part,' he was saying, 'but I always found Aggie's tales fascinating and I thought they would make good reading—especially with Rose doing the illustrations— and, according to the publisher, they do!' There was satisfaction in his voice.

'Did you always want to write?'

He chuckled. 'My mother says I had her writing down my stories before I could even print. I've written magazine articles and such over the years, but it's only recently that I felt the time was right to try a book.'

'Are you going to write more of the same?' She could stand like this for ever.

'No—at least,' he amended, 'not right away. I want to try a mystery next—with West Coast setting, of course. Now,' he said, suddenly releasing his hold on her shoulders, 'I'm going to make some notes and take some more pictures. Get some driftwood for a fire, will you? Make sure it's dry,' he added absently, already absorbed.

'Aye, aye, Captain.' She saluted him with a slightly mocking smile and left him in peace.

It didn't take long to stack a pile of wood ready for a

fire. Jesse was still scribbling in his notebook, so Stefanie explored the tiny beach, pocketing some pretty shells and pieces of cold water coral. Catching a flash of green from the corner of her eye, she bent down and released a glass ball from its tangled nest of seaweed.

'Look, Jesse!' she exclaimed, holding it out on the palm of her hand. 'A crystal ball!'

'It's a float cut loose from a Japanese fishing net,' Jesse explained prosaically, tucking his notebook away and coming towards her.

'It's a crystal ball,' Stefanie said firmly, wiping it clean on her jeans. She held it up and peered into it.

He smiled with lazy amusement. 'Okay—it's a crystal ball. So tell me, can you see our future in its wondrous depths, O gypsy queen?'

Our future. She heard the words with a seriousness she knew he didn't intend. Is there to be an 'our' future, or just your future and my future? she thought. She had a sudden and fervent wish to see just what did lie in store for her; to know if she was more than a somewhat amusing neighbour with whom Jesse was willing to idle away a few hours. She looked up to find him regarding her thoughtfully. 'I—it doesn't work,' she said hastily. 'I guess it's broken. Here,' she added, thrusting it at him. 'Keep it for me, please. My pockets aren't big enough.' Managing a rather wobbly smile, she turned away from his intent grey eyes. She had an uncomfortable suspicion that she had given away something just then, and quickly she started to gather more wood, giving herself time to pull together.

As she turned away, Jesse put the small float in one of his voluminous pockets, frowning slightly. He watched her for a few moments and then, with a shrug, touched a match to crumpled paper and added pieces of wood until there was a sizeable blaze on the quiet little beach.

When Stefanie returned with her armload of wood, he was filling a blackened kettle with water from a canteen. 'How about some lunch?' he asked casually after a quick look at her face. 'I know it's early yet, but . . .'

'You brought lunch? Great! What are we having?'

Jesse chuckled. 'Mention food and you light up like a Christmas tree!'

'So I get hungry—what are we having?'

'Hang on a minute—if you can—and you'll find out.' He took a pot from a small box on the boat and placed it on the coals of the fire to heat. He then spread a blanket on the sand and put out a loaf of rye bread, cheese and some fruit.

Stefanie watched impatiently for a moment, then risked a peep in the pot. 'Chilli!' she exclaimed. 'I love chilli! I hope it's hot. Did you make it?'

'I made it—and it's hot enough to make your eyes water,' Jesse answered, and handed her a ladle. 'Stir.'

'Yes, sir!' It was fun again. The unreasonable tension she had felt a short time ago had vanished. It was a relief.

'Ooh—that was good,' Stefanie said later as she wiped the last of the chilli sauce from her bowl with a piece of bread. 'I couldn't eat another thing!'

'Small wonder,' Jesse said mildly. 'You had two bowlsful—and I do mean full. But who's counting?'

She wrinkled her nose at him. 'It's entirely your fault for being such a good cook.'

'I am, aren't I?' he agreed smugly. 'Have a banana.'

She shook her head. 'Maybe later. Do we do the dishes here or pack them home dirty?'

He smothered a yawn. 'I vote for dirty. We've got about an hour before we have to head back. I think,' he said, stretching out on the blanket with his hands behind his head, 'I'll snooze,' His eyes closed.

Stefanie stifled a sigh. Ignored again, she thought gloomily. Suppressing an urge to cuddle up beside him on the blanket, she rinsed the dishes in the ocean and neatly repacked the remainder of the lunch.

Not wanting to just sit and stare at him while he slept—and not quite daring to lie down beside him—she perched on one of the rocks edging the tiny cove. She savoured the freshness of the moist air with its mingled odours of cedar, salt and seaward. It had been a long time since she had been in such a remote spot. There were no houses, no roads, not even a jet stream to remind her of the modern world. She shifted around to look yet again at the totem poles, and at that moment a bald eagle and its mate flew low overhead, their black wings lazily stroking the air. How suitable to see them here, Stefanie thought, knowing only too well that the eagle was disappearing as fast as the untamed wilderness it symbolised. She watched as they flew out of sight, relishing the solitude, and then, unable to resist his presence any longer, she went quietly back to Jesse.

She stood for a long moment gazing down at the rugged face relaxed in sleep. She wanted desperately to kneel beside him to smooth the tangle of glossy beard around his lips and wanted desperately to again feel the touch of their firm softness on hers. Dropping down suddenly, she sat cross-legged on the edge of the blanket and stared broodingly out over the water.

Since the fiasco after the dance he had given no indication that he wanted their relationship to be other than what it always had been—affectionately platonic. Even this morning, she thought, I was the one who wanted more, not him. She remembered how quick he had been to withdraw from her arms. She felt a wave of depression wash over her and turned to look at him, but there were no clues to be found in his sleeping countenance. She turned back to her study of the ocean, a frown marring the smoothness of her brow.

He must be in love with Louisa, she thought with pain. A sudden all too clear picture of the petite but curvaceous blonde flashed before her, leaving a bitter taste in her mouth as it faded. She scowled at the memory, jabbing a stick into the sand in frustration.

There was only one way to find out how he felt about Louisa—ask. But as much as she needed to hear the truth, she was simply too much of a coward to ask. Wondering, with a grimace of disgust, what had happened to the straightforwardness she had always prided herself on, Stefanie turned to Jesse again, to find his eyes open and focused on her.

'About time you woke up,' she muttered crossly,

using her too willing anger to hide the fluster caused by his unexpected scrutiny.

'Cranky, aren't you?' Jesse gathered his long legs under him and stood up, stretching lithely. 'Maybe you should have had the nap.'

'I'd just like to get going,' she frowned as she stood up brushing damp sand from her palms. She'd had enough. It was too wearing to be with him like this, wanting—needing—more than he could give. 'Let's go.'

'What's wrong?' He was obviously puzzled by the change in her.

'Nothing,' she said shortly.

Jesse regarded her stony face. 'Very well,' he said coolly. 'We'll go. It's time anyway.'

Silence stretched between them as they loaded the boat and set out. Stefanie knew she was being unreasonable, but perversely clung to her resentment. Jesse, after a perplexed look at her peevish profile, shrugged and ignored her. The relaxed and friendly atmosphere of the journey in was gone.

The air felt heavier and caught at the throb of the engine until the sound surrounded them. The misty clouds cloaking the hillsides crept in closer. Scattered fingers of fog swirled above the water and slowly began to wrap them with blank whiteness.

Stefanie clutched the sides of her seat with growing fear. 'Jesse—we'll get l-lost!' It was terrifying to think of them adrift in the tiny boat at the mercy of the ocean's power.

Jesse's smile was brief. 'Don't worry,' he assured her over the putt-putt of the all but idling engine. 'We'll head for shore.'

It seemed to take forever before they felt the bow nudge sandy shore. Stefanie jumped out quickly and pulled the boat safely on to the beach, heartily glad to be on firm ground. 'Will—will we have to spend the night?' she asked as soon as Jesse had beached the boat.

'Looks that way,' Jesse answered with a tight smile. 'Sure you can put up with me that long?'

'I guess I'll have to.' She knew her tone was too flat.

He whirled around, his face cut by a deep frown.

'Listen, Stefanie, this isn't my idea of a good time either, but we're stuck here, at least until morning. Now,' he continued angrily, 'make yourself useful while I radio Tom before he has the Coastguard out after us. Get some firewood,' he commanded harshly, 'and quit sulking!'

'I'm not!' Stefanie protested, but he had already turned back to the boat and was hauling a chest from the bow.

The feeling of depression stayed with her as she braved the fog to search the high-tide line for chunks of driftwood. She knew she was behaving badly and wondered why. Petulance wasn't her nature. Jesse had done nothing to deserve the antagonism she was feeling. He was behaving perfectly—for a friend. And that was the problem, she realised miserably as she dropped another armload on the growing pile of firewood.

Finished, she sat on a log watching Jesse as he expertly lit the fire. The quick crackling flames did much to dispel the errie gloom of the fog, but Stefanie knew it was going to be a long and very cold night unless she made an effort to get a grip on her emotions. She sighed and began with an apology.

'Jesse,' she said in a small voice. 'I've been behaving badly. I'm sorry.'

He turned from his crouched position by the growing fire, his eyes narrow as they regarded her closely. 'Is it something I did?'

She stared steadfastly into the fire. 'No,' she said. 'I was just being—silly.' This was not the time to ask about his involvement with Louisa. She had all night. She looked up with a tentative smile. 'I'm sorry,' he repeated softly.

'Accepted.' The word was brief, but the grey eyes definitely softened. 'Lend me a hand, will you? Let's get this camp ship-shape.'

'Aye, aye, Captain!' Stefanie stood up quickly, determined to be cheerful. 'What's first?'

She helped him carry the chest from the boat to the fire. In it was all they would need to make themselves as comfortable as possible in the circumstances.

'I like to be prepared,' Jesse explained as he opened the chest. 'I often spend a night out in the summer, and,' he concluded, 'emergencies do happen.' He pulled an old tobacco tin containing fishing line and hooks from the chest. 'Can you manage here? I'm going to jig for cod off the rocks. I won't be far,' he hastened to add. 'Just a few yards away.'

'I'll manage,' Stefanie smiled, and waved him off, ready now to enter into the adventure. It was surprisingly easy to slip back into camp life. She unpacked the chest, finding, to her satisfaction, cooking utensils as well as basic cooking ingredients.

She fuelled the fire with chunks of thick flat bark that Jesse had told her earlier came from the Douglas fir tree. They provided a good base of hot coals and she found some flat rocks to place around the blaze. Pushing up the sleeves of her parka, she quickly mixed flour, baking powder and lard together, adding water until she got the right consistency needed for bannock. She kneaded the dough and put it in a large pan on a rock in the fire. Surrounded by the heat of the glowing coals, it would cook quite evenly.

Stefanie had the camp well under control by the time Jesse returned with his string of cod. The contents of the chest were stacked neatly to one side and the chest itself was ready to be used as a table. Logs had been pulled closer to the fire to serve as backrests and seats.

'Well, well,' Jesse drawled, his swift grey eyes taking it all in. 'And I thought I was going to have to take care of you!'

'If it'll make you feel any better,' Stefanie smiled sweetly, 'you can get more wood. We're going to need a lot more before morning.'

'And who'll take care of these?' He held up the still flopping fish.

Stefanie reached for them. 'Me, I guess. Not,' she hastened to add, 'that I believe in division of labour or anything, but I may as well finish the cooking having gone this far.'

Jesse looked doubtful. 'They do have to be cleaned, you know.'

'No kidding,' she said, wrinkling her nose in light sarcasm. 'Go get the wood, will you?'

With a slight shrug and an amused grin, Jesse gave her a mock salute and disappeared into the fog.

Cleaning fish wasn't a task she enjoyed, but she did it quickly and surely, laying the neat fillets on a plate beside her. Finished, she scrubbed her hands in the icy brine to remove all traces of fishy smell.

By the time Jesse had gathered a good-sized pile of wood, supper was almost ready. Fish was sizzling, coffee was brewing and the bannock had cooked perfectly, crisp and golden brown. 'Almost done,' Stefanie said with satisfaction. 'Hungry?'

He dropped a final armload of wood. 'Starved,' he admitted. Unnoticed by her, his eyes were tender as he watched her kneeling by the fire deftly transferring flaky cod fillets to waiting plates. 'You really did grow up in the bush, didn't you?'

'Right smack dab in the middle,' Stefanie replied with a flushed grin. 'Let's eat.'

After the tasty meal they cleaned up and then lingered around the fire with warming mugs of coffee. The actual temperature of the night was not that low, but the fog's touch was chilling and damp. They kept the fire hot, enjoying its brightness in the dark night. Sometimes they would talk or laugh, sometimes they would sit in comfortable silence. Stefanie was strongly aware of just how right it felt to be with him.

As though reading her mind, Jesse turned to her with a warm smile. 'You're a good person to be marooned with, Stefanie Hart.'

'Because I can clean fish?' she asked teasingly, feeling a warm glow around her heart.

'Because,' he said with soft but unmistakable admiration, 'you made the best of what a lot of people would consider a bad situation. And because,' he added with his lopsided grin, 'you didn't blame me for falling asleep and not getting us back before the fog set in!'

'I'd forgotten about that!' Stefanie admitted. 'If I wasn't enjoying myself, I'd really light into you!'

'Are you enjoying yourself?'

She nodded. 'Sure—at least, right now. I don't know how I'm going to feel after sitting up all night in this damp.' She yawned delicately. 'It's going to be a long night.'

'We do have a sleeping bag,' Jesse said, watching her closely. 'We'll have to share, but it'll be warmer that way—sharing body heat.'

'Sharing . . . y-yes, I guess it would be—be warmer.' She strived to remain cool, but knew to her chagrin that he missed nothing of sudden confusion in her eyes nor the blush that heated her cheeks. Silently she cursed herself for being so—so damned virginal!

'Oh, Stefanie,' he said softly, touching her face with gentle fingers. 'It's nothing to be ashamed of.'

'W-what?' she blinked at him, her eyes round.

'Being a virgin,' he stated simply. 'You are, aren't you?'

'Y-yes.'

He seemed to hesitate for a moment as though searching for words. 'Is—is that the reason you were so frightened the other night? Or was there something else?'

She nodded, staring down at the hands she had clasped tightly around her knees, nibbling nervously on her bottom lip.

His fingers held her chin and he raised her head until she had to look at him. 'Can you tell me about it?' His voice was soft, his grey eyes unbelievingly tender.

'I—I'd like to,' she whispered, her eyelashes sweeping down to fan on her cheeks, 'but—but . . .' Helplessly her voice broke off. She felt Jesse's arm curve around her shoulders and went without resistance into their shelter.

'Take your time. We've got all night.' His voice was calmly reassuring, as was his touch, and Stefanie knew that, for the first time, she could share the horrifying experience that had held her caged for so long. Struggling against the reticence of years, she began to speak, her voice a hesitant thread of sound.

'I used to spend the summers in camp with Dad. The year when I was f-fifteen, there was a new man, younger than usual. I—we got along quite well. I guess I had a crush on him.' She stopped and drew a deep breath before she plunged on, her voice muffled against Jesse's chest. 'He kissed me one day—my first kiss,' she added bitterly. 'I—I liked it at first, but—but he wouldn't stop. He turned—vile, when I pleaded with him. He tore my clothes and hit me and—and forced me ...' Her voice choked off, her shoulders shaking in Jesse's tight hold.

'Did he rape you?' Jesse's voice was harsh. Her disjointed and shaky words had given him an all too vivid picture of what had happened. He felt a surge of violent anger against the man who had forced his brutal lust on an unsuspecting girl.

'It was as close to rape as it could be without—without ...' Stefanie broke off and then continued flatly, 'Dad came back unexpectedly. He beat the hell out of him. After I recovered—physically—I was sent to school in Winnipeg. I felt like I was being punished. No one ever said anything about it—Dad couldn't even look me in the face for a long time afterwards. I—I felt like it was my fault!' She stopped, realising for the first time that her father's withdrawal had been caused by his own guilt, not because he blamed her. The last of her own guilt fled, and with rather a shaky smile she looked at Jesse.

'God, Stefanie, what a terrible time that was for you!' There was anger underlying his words. 'You should have been experiencing nothing more than a few gentle kisses—not dealing with brutal lust!' The hand that stroked her hair trembled slightly. 'It makes me doubly ashamed of my behaviour the other night. Can you forgive me?'

'I have,' she whispered. 'If I hadn't played that stupid little trick about my age, you would never have been so—so angry.' She sighed. It was a relief to have him know what had happened, but she wanted to tell him more; tell him how she had come alive in his arms, how he had awakened her woman's desires. She wanted desperately to tell him how very much she loved him, but there was something she had to know first.

'Jesse,' she began tentatively from the circle of his arms, 'can I—can I ask you something?'

'Yes, of course. What is it?'

'Aggie told me about—about . . .'

'About Wanda?' Jesse interrupted over her hesitation. 'I thought she might have.'

Stefanie frowned and stirred restlessly. She had some curiosity about his dead wife, yes—but it was the very much alive Louisa who concerned her. Before she could correct his assumption, he started to talk, his deep voice rumbling under her ear.

'Wanda and I were high school sweethearts,' he explained matter-of-factly. 'We married right after graduation—over our parents' objections, I might add. If we'd waited a year like they wanted us to . . . Well, we thought we knew best. We started university together, but before long we were fast going our separate ways—there was a whole new world to experience and . . .' She felt his shrug. 'There was one point when we might have made it work, but she——' He hesitated for a moment. 'Let's just say she did something I couldn't forgive and it was all over. She died a few months later.' He shook his head. 'It was a long time ago. Sometimes it feels like another lifetime.' There was a sharp edge of regret in his voice.

'Did you love her a lot?' Was that the attraction Louisa held for him—that she reminded him of Wanda?

'Oh yes—for a while. We just—grew out of it. We didn't have the maturity needed to work things out. Needless to say,' he finished dryly, 'I'm now a strong opponent of teenage marriages!'

They were quiet for a few moments. Stefanie searched for the words she wanted, but before she could say anything, he gave her shoulders a quick squeeze and stood up to throw wood on the fire, and the opportunity was lost. The question of Louisa remained unanswered.

Stefanie stifled an impatient sigh as she watched him move with lithe grace around the fire, setting up for the night. She knew he liked her—that much was obvious.

But other than the night of the dance he had treated her with kindness and concern as though he regarded her as nothing more than a friend. It's not fair, she thought glumly, all he has to do is look at me and my knees wobble. And as far as he's concerned, I'm just another one of his lame ducks!

'Aha!' She looked up at Jesse's exclamation. 'Here it is.' He pulled a small bottle from the chest and added some to the coffee in their mugs. 'Brandy,' he explained, handing her mug to her. 'Purely medicinal, of course.'

'Of course,' Stefanie agreed. 'Here's to medicine!' It was easy to appreciate the warm rush of the liquor in the chill dampness of the foggy night. She drank quickly and held out her mug for another. Let Jesse quirk his eyebrows. It was going to be a long night.

She knew it was going to be even longer when she saw the narrowness of the sleeping bag stretched out on the sand. Gulping her drink nervously, she wondered how she was going to be able to hide her feelings stretched out beside him in the intimate confines of that sleeping bag. The very thought of pressing against his long length caused her heart to beat faster and her limbs to quiver.

'Don't worry, Stefanie.' Jesse was watching her closely, his smile reassuring. 'Nothing will happen.'

She managed a brief smile and nodded. Needing a breathing space, she hurried away from the fire, her retreating figure followed by narrowed grey eyes.

'Take off your jacket,' Jesse advised a short time later as she sat on the edge of the sleeping bag to remove her boots. 'It'll be warmer—and roomier!'

There was little enough room to be had even without the bulky jackets. Annoyed at the trepidation she was feeling, Stefanie fought to remain calm as she wriggled in beside him. He had promised nothing would happen, and that was the problem—she had to hide her desire because he felt none.

It wasn't easy. In the narrowness of the sleeping bag, her cheek rested on his shoulder, her hand on his chest. Her hips pressed against his and one knee fell over his long legs. She bit her lip hard as his arm came up around her shoulders.

'Comfy?'

'Y-yes.' It was an outright lie. Comfortable was the last word she would use to describe what she was feeling.

'Stefanie—relax! Nothing's going to happen.' His hand smoothed the hair back from her forehead. 'Relax,' he whispered, and began to talk. In the fog-bound remoteness of the tiny island, he told her tales of Aggie's people in a simple but colourful narrative. With her head pressed against the sensuous rumble of his voice, Stefanie slowly did the impossible. She relaxed, and then finally slept.

Some time during the night she stirred, slowly becoming aware of the man beside her. With her cheek still pressed to his chest, she could feel his slow regular breathing and the steady beat of his heart. It was a warm feeling of security that cocooned her from the surrounding darkness. Langourously she rubbed a lazy hand over the rough wool of his sweater and then slipped her fingers under it, stroking the satiny muscles of his chest. As her fingers slid down to lightly knead the hard flatness of his stomach, she felt a sharp intake of breath and knew he was awake.

'Jesse,' she murmured, and raised her head from his shoulder, moving her lips over the crispness of his beard to touch his mouth. With a muffled groan, he tightened his arms around her and with a sudden motion pulled her on top of him, his mouth covering hers with shocking urgency. Her body melted easily against his, every nerve ending acutely aware of his male hardness. He tugged impatiently at her sweater and pulled it up until he could touch the soft roundness of the breasts that crushed against his chest. His hands moved over her bare skin, running down her back to pull her hips impossibly closer to his. He devoured the moan of desire that quivered on her lips and she stiffened with the exquisite tension of passion, breathing his name over and over as her body demanded release.

She felt a shudder run through him and his hand

gripped her shoulders painfully. Then, with shocking suddenness, he thrust her away from him and in a lithe motion was out of the sleeping bag, standing tall above her in the dark.

'That's enough!' he ground out savagely. 'Go back to sleep!' Without another word, he shoved his arms into his parka, pulled on his boots and walked away into the fog.

Too stunned to even move, Stefanie stared in the direction he had taken. Her body, minutes before quivering with desire, began to shake from the pain of his rejection. Curling into a tight ball, she pushed a clenched fist against her mouth in a vain attempt to stop the tears that scalded her icy cheeks. She didn't move again, not even when he finally returned. From her huddled position, she watched him build up the fire, watched while he sat as far from her as he could to stare broodingly into the flames, and knew he would rather spend what was left of the night sitting in the cold damp than come back to her. What's wrong with me? The tortured words echoed in her benumbed mind over and over until she slipped into an uneasy sleep.

It was light when she awoke again. The fog had lifted during the night, but the clouds hung low, moisture seeping from their sullen greyness. Stiff and uncomfortably damp, Stefanie got up slowly, feeling as sullen as the day itself. Where was Jesse?

He came from the trees that lined the beach just as she was pulling on her boots. His face was as cold and withdrawn as it must have been last night after he had rejected her offer of love. Biting her lip, Stefanie bent her head to tug at the knot in her bootlace, missing his flicker of pain at the sight of her pale and tear-swollen face.

'Get ready,' he said without expression. 'We're leaving.' He began to load the boat.

Except for a few curt commands, he was silent all the way back to Tofino. Feeling totally dejected, Stefanie used all her strength to maintain a calm façade. How had the warm intimacy of last night turned into the icy distance she saw every time she dared to look at him?

Her heart ached at the knowledge that she had ruined everything by wanting more from their relationship than he wanted to give.

Last evening he had been kind and understanding, a friend she had trusted enough to reveal, for the first time, the tortured secret of her past. This morning he was a cold and withdrawn stranger. It hurt—badly.

It was a relief to reach her place at last. Anger at Jesse's continued coldness grew with her pain in a potentially volatile mixture. She wanted desperately to be alone. She knew she couldn't take much more, and if she did explode . . .

'Thank you very much,' she said with sarcastic emphasis as she climbed out of his truck. 'It was most—entertaining!' She slammed the door hard before he could say anything and watched with clenched fists as he tore away, spraying gravel behind him.

Her anger began to dissipate as soon as he was out of sight. Feeling very depressed, Stefanie fumbled for her keys with tear-glazed eyes and let herself in. She released the yowling cat from the confines of the utility room, ignoring his incessant purrs of gratitude. Filling his dish, she put it out on the step. 'There,' she absently, 'have a picnic.'

Wearily she climbed the stairs to her room, stripped off her damp clothes and went to shower. She stood under the hot spray until it began to cool, tears adding to the wetness on her face. Scarcely bothering to dry herself, she slipped into her bed and fell quickly asleep.

It was late afternoon when she woke up. As she lay in bed, reluctant to get up, she remembered suddenly that Jim had said he would come over Monday night. Had he been serious, or was it just said to get a rise out of Jesse? Jesse . . . With a grimace of pain, Stefanie pushed back the covers and climbed out of bed.

Wondering whether or not she should expect Jim, she dressed in a wrap-around denim skirt and a dusky rose cotton blouse. As she applied make-up to hide the dark circles under her eyes, she found herself hoping that he would show up. She had felt a quick liking for him, and had a sudden longing for his straightforward and undemanding company.

She hadn't been dressed long when she heard a knock at the door. It was Jim. Her smile was wide and genuine as she opened the door. 'Come in, Jim—it's good to see you!'

'Hi, Stef!' Jim's voice was cheerful. 'I wasn't sure if I should show up or not—I can get lost if you want.'

'No way!' She took him by the arm and pulled him in. 'I'm glad you're here—I need the company.'

'Good. I know it's early, but I thought we could cook up these salmon steaks.' He handed her a paper bag. 'Caught today, I might add.' He looked at her with a raised eyebrow. 'Is that all right—you don't have other plans?'

'Not a one, and your idea is perfect.' Stefanie was feeling warmer than she had all day. 'I haven't eaten yet—and I'm starving!' To her surprise, it was true.

'I also brought some wine,' said Jim, holding up a bottle. 'I—er—feel like celebrating.'

'Celebrating what?' She took the bottle and uncorked it.

He grinned as he leaned against the counter. 'I heard today that I'm being transferred—back to Saskatchewan! Much as I like it out here, I'll be glad to go back home.'

'I'm glad for you, Jim.' Stefanie handed him a glass of wine. 'When are you leaving?'

'In two weeks,' he said. 'They aren't wasting any time.'

His fair face was wreathed with such a happy smile that Stefanie asked with sudden insight, 'Is that all we're celebrating—your posting?'

'Well, no,' he grinned again, rather sheepishly this time. 'I phoned Carly—my girl—this afternoon to tell her and—well, we're going to get married this summer!'

'Congratulations!' A sharp pang clouded her eyes for a brief second, but she refused to be glum in the face of his obvious happiness. She raised her glass to him and smiled seriously. 'I hope you'll both be very happy, Jim.'

'Thanks, Stef.' He hesitated briefly. 'You and Jess . . .?'

'Don't ask,' she interrupted hastily, turning away from his astute eyes.

'Okay, Stefanie,' Jim said quietly, touching her shoulder. 'But if you ever need to talk——'

'I need to eat,' she said with forced brightness. 'Does your offer of food come complete with cooking, or is that up to me?'

'Both of us,' he said promptly, following her lead. 'I brought the makings for a mean salad—you take care of that and I'll see to the salmon. Deal?'

'Deal!'

Jim's happiness slowly lifted her spirits. Her cheerfulness became less and less forced as they joked through the cooking and she ate the delicious meal with a good appetite. By the time they sat in front of the fire with coffee and cognac, she was feeling truly mellow. It was such a relief after the day's earlier tension.

Jim sorted through her record collection, pulling out a pile of what he called oldies but goodies, and they chatted away to the music of the Beatles, the Stones, Dylan . . .

Jim talked a lot about Carly and their plans for the future. Stefanie listened patiently, realising how frustrating it must be for him to spend this exciting time so many miles from the woman he loved. If it was me, she reflected, I'd need him . . . him. In her mind's eye she saw Jesse as clearly as if he was standing before her. Angrily she shook her head to chase away the image, but the imprint had been made. Her hard-won relaxation vanished swiftly and she felt a moody restlessness take over. She was more than a little glad to hear Jim say he had to leave.

'I've got a couple of reports to write up,' he explained as he unwound from his position on the hearth.

Stefanie followed him to the kitchen. 'I had a good time, Jim. Thanks for coming over.'

'My pleasure,' he smiled. 'And, Stefanie—thanks for listening. About Carly and the wedding, I mean.'

'Any time—I enjoyed hearing about her.' She smiled at him as he opened the door to leave and said sincerely, 'I think she's a lucky girl, Jim.'

He flushed, his brown eyes alight with pleasure. 'Thanks, Stef. Goodnight.'

Reaching up impulsively, she planted a quick kiss on his mouth. 'Goodnight, Jim. See you.'

'See you,' he echoed, and went to his car.

Stefanie shut the door and leaned against it for a long moment. It's not fair, she thought woefully. Jim can successfully conduct his love life with over a thousand miles between him and Carly—and I can't even manage the man next door! Feeling deflated without Jim's happiness to draw upon, she wandered listlessly into the living room. It was far too early for bed, especially after sleeping most of the day. Unable to sit, she stood at the window with her glass in her hand, staring pensively into the dark night.

His soft knock was not heard over the music. He let himself in quietly and stood in the doorway between kitchen and living room. He had waited until Jim had driven away, knowing that in spite of his genuine liking for the other man, his resentment would be too strong to hide. His lips tightened as his narrowed eyes saw the remains of an intimate dinner, the scattered records near the stereo, the half empty decanter of cognac on the hearth . . .

'Stefanie . . .' He spoke with a harshness that surprised even him, and she whirled around from the window. Her startled expression was quickly replaced by one of anger.

'Why in the hell can't you knock!' she exploded, shaking drops of spilled drink from her fingers.

'I did,' Jesse said with chilling remoteness.

'In future, I suggest you either wait for an answer, or—or go home!'

'What's the matter?' he taunted. 'Did lover boy leave you—frustrated?'

Stefanie winced at the cruelty of the words, and called on an inner strength for control. She raised her glass to her lips and slowly drew the last of the cognac into her mouth, looking at him over the rim with limpid eyes. 'As a matter of fact,' she said, her lips curving into a secretive smile, 'we had a very—nice time.' She quickly put down the glass to hide trembling hands.

Jesse's long stride brought him across the room, his eyes smouldering in a growing heat of anger. His hands shot out to grab her shoulders in a biting grip and he pulled her hard against his chest. He glared down at her, his lips taut as they began to descend. 'I'll show you—nice!'

'Why are you so mad at me?' She could not hide her pain.

The soft unexpected words penetrated his anger as no protestations would have. Jesse straightened abruptly and stared into her eyes. He saw no fear, not even a trace of the anger she had every right to feel. Instead he saw an infinite sadness in the beautiful misted green. He cursed in self-loathing and dropped his hands, turning away from her. 'I'm sorry,' he said stiffly.

Stefanie saw his hands clench for control. She looked at him intently, a fine line of pain etched on her brow. 'Why, Jesse?' she repeated in a troubled voice. 'Why are you mad at me?'

He shook his head as he ran his fingers through his rumpled curls. He exhaled a long breath as though trying to expel his anger. 'I'm not mad at you, Stefanie,' he managed to say evenly.

'You do a damn good imitation of it,' she retorted. Still studying him, her eyes narrow and reflective, she asked, 'What's wrong?'

He shrugged, his mouth breaking into a rueful smile. 'Be damned if I know.'

Stefanie scowled in exasperation, determined to have it out. 'Either something is wrong,' she insisted, 'or you're awfully damned moody—and either way I don't like it. We're supposed to be—to be friends. Tell me why you're mad at me.'

'It's not you I'm mad at—more at myself for . . .' He stopped.

'For what, Jesse?' She was softly insistent.

His eyes were hooded and his face withdrawn as he looked at her. 'For wanting to make love to you.'

She drew a sharp breath at the impact of the

unexpected words. 'And—and that makes you angry?'
She calmly forced the words passed the hammering of
her heart.

He turned to stare out into the blackness of the night.
'It makes me angry that I'm tempted to—to tempt you.'

'Would that be so very bad?'

He didn't move from his position at the window. 'For
you, yes. You should wait for love,' he said remotely.
'It wouldn't be fair to deny you that.'

Stefanie closed her eyes at the sharp stab of pain. His
meaning was only too clear. He wants me but he
doesn't love me, she thought in despair. She blinked
rapidly to keep back the tears, staring at his stiffly held
back. His desire and her love—was it enough? It was
her decision.

She knew for certain now that she could love—really
love a man in all senses of the word. And she knew with
equal sureness that it had to be this man who, however
unconsciously, had awakened her. She took a tentative
step towards him and stopped, wishing she could be as
sure of him as she was about herself.

As she hesitated, she suddenly remembered last night
and the hunger with which his mouth had devoured
hers, remembered how he had trembled at the touch of
her hands. Had his withdrawal been because he had
promised her nothing would happen? At this moment the
answer was clear. Trusting her instincts, she went to him
and laid her hand lightly on his shoulder. 'Jesse . . .'

He turned and looked at her, his mouth unsmiling,
his eyes brooding.

'Jesse,' she said again, her eyes unconsciously
pleading. 'Kiss me.' The words were softer than a
breath of air.

Jesse groaned and caught her to him, his fingers
entwining in the length of her hair. 'I don't think I
could stop with a kiss.'

Stefanie closed her eyes and exhaled slowly. 'I don't
want you to.'

'Stefanie,' he whispered hoarsely, his thumbs rubbing
her shoulders, heating the skin beneath the thin cotton
of her blouse. 'You don't know what you're asking!'

'Oh yes, I do,' she said with a sudden dimpling smile, reaching up to run her hand over the crispness of his beard. 'At least,' she amended seriously, 'I think I do.' She wrapped her arms around his neck and pressed her body to his. 'Show me, Jesse,' she whispered.

He groaned deep in his chest, his hands convulsively clutching at her willing body, but still he held back. 'I can't, Stefanie—I shouldn't!'

'Don't you want me?' She pouted slightly, moulding her pliant body even closer to his.

'You know damned well I do, witch,' he growled, running his hands over her back and staring at her softly parted lips. 'But you . . .'

Stefanie shook her head, gently laying a finger on his lips, inhaling sharply as his tongue touched its tip. She swallowed and tried to tell him that it was all right, but it was hard to speak coherently. Her body ached at the closeness of his, her senses swam with his warm man scent and all she wanted to do was answer the desire she saw in his eyes. 'Oh hell, Jesse,' she swore with a soft moan. 'Just kiss me!'

With great restraint his lips touched hers. Stefanie felt the hesitancy behind the kiss, felt the control of his stiffly held body, and knew he was giving her time to draw back. With an impatient whimper, she curled her fingers in his hair and her tongue darted out to trace the outline of his mouth, delicately insisting that he relinquish control.

But when he answered her challenge, it was she who lost control. Helplessly she clung to him, inflamed by the probing onslaught of his mouth. What she had thought was need before paled to insignificance as wave after wave of passion washed over her. Her body was as malleable as heated metal as Jesse pulled her hips against the tautness of his. And then, with shocking suddenness, his lips left hers.

'There,' he said thickly, 'I kissed you. Satisfied?'

Stefanie stared at him, her eyes wide and incredulous. 'No!' she moaned, burying her burning face in his neck. 'God, no! Don't tease, Jesse,' she begged. She couldn't bear to have him turn away now.

'I'm not, sweetheart,' he muttered against her ruby-bright hair. 'But you must be sure.'

If there had been any lingering fear or doubt, it vanished, and Stefanie's heart swelled with love. She knew by the tightness of his body and the rapid beating of his heart under her cheek that he was exercising great restraint to give her one last chance. She lifted her face and leaned back against the iron circle of his arms and smiled tremulously. 'I am sure, Jesse,' she said clearly. 'So very, very sure.' Her eyes held his and their message was clear.

I love you. I want you to teach me the joys of love. I want to lie in your arms and feel your skin against mine; to taste you as you taste me; to move with the touch of your body against mine. 'I need you, Jesse,' she whispered.

In slow motion his head lowered and he touched his mouth to hers. His kiss this time was slow and drugging, promising her gentleness and understanding. When he lifted his head to look at her again, she smiled joyfully. Secure in her love and trust, she knew only anticipation as he led her to a nest of cushions in front of the fire. They stood with their arms around each other, until, with a growing urgency, Jesse tightened his hold and kissed her until her senses swam and her body rocked against his.

Tearing his mouth from hers, he kissed across her cheek, caressing the satiny skin under her ear with the tip of his tongue, and she gasped and squirmed with the exquisite pain that coursed through her to coil in her loins. Impatient fingers unbuttoned her blouse and tugged at it until her breasts were bared to his hungry eyes.

'Beautiful,' he murmured. 'You are so beautiful, my sweet Stefanie.' His hands cupped her throbbing breasts and with a shaky sigh he bent to kiss each tip. His tongue and teeth gently teased each nipple into harder peaks of arousal, teasing, tickling, tonguing over and over until she cried out in an agony of desire. Clutching his head in her hands, she raised it until she could touch her parted lips to his. His fingers tugged at her skirt until it fell on the floor between them and she wrapped her arms around him as his strong hands pulled her hips to the tight fit of his.

Groaning, Jesse tore his lips from hers long enough to lower her to the cushions on the floor. Stefanie lay still, her hair a fiery flame on the sheepskins. Jesse looked at her with smouldering eyes as the firelight danced over her body, turning the cream of her skin to gold, glowing on her curving hips and highlighting the breasts that still throbbed from his kisses. With a little sound, she held out her arms, begging him to come closer.

Kneeling in front of her, he gave her a quick reassuring kiss, unbuttoned his shirt and cast it impatiently aside. Stefanie watched shamelessly as he stripped, the tip of her tongue wetting her swollen lips, then gasped with wonder as his lean hard body was exposed to the flickering firelight.

Jesse bent slowly over her, moistly kissing her breast, her stomach, her thighs. He slid his hands under her hips and removed her panties with ease so there was no barrier to his seeking lips. Stefanie moaned, helplessly arching under the simmering power of his intimate kisses. His tongue stroked and lingered on her sensitive skin, then retraced its downward path with patient ardour until he lay full length beside her, his mouth covering hers with the erotic taste of her own body.

Stefanie turned fervently to him, her caresses matching his, urgently seeking, stroking. He murmured endearments and words of passion with ragged breath, kissing her lips, her neck, her breasts until her desire became a frenzy.

She moaned his name, her whispers becoming pleas. Moving slowly, he took her then, his eyes burning with restrained passion. Enveloped by her heat, he waited, murmuring reassuringly as he kissed and caressed her, until she instinctively moved with the ageless rhythm of need. Sensuously he moved with her, leading her on a searing spiral of passion. She cried out his name and clutched his shoulders tightly as the pinpoint of ectasy grew stronger, brighter and then exploded into a million flashing lights. Groaning with the force of his own release, Jesse pulled her hard against him and she lay panting and incredulous in his arms.

'My God,' she whispered, burying her face into the warm skin of his shoulder. 'I never thought it could be like that! It was—was . . .'

'Beautiful,' he finished for her. One hand stroked her shining hair while the other pressed her close against him. 'It was . . . special, sweetheart.'

'Yes—I know.' Her voice was low and husky. He had made it so. She knew instinctively that he had used considerable restraint to make it good for her. His lovemaking had been incredibly sensuous and erotic, allowing selflessly for her inexperience. Her eyes roved softly over the magnificence of his reclining body, her fingers stroking his velvet hardness. How she loved this man!

Suddenly her senses were again filled with him. She became acutely aware of the heaviness of his legs as they lay entwined with his. Her nostrils flared slightly as the heated scent of their lovemaking washed over her. As her love for him rose, so did a fierce joy, and she knew just how right it was to be here with him like this. She turned until she was reclining on top of him, her lips tremulous, smiling her love. Whatever pain might lie in the future, tonight he was hers.

She squirmed around until she sat straddling his hips and stretched sensuously. She gasped as his hands came up quickly to stroke the coral nipples that thrust through wine dark strands of hair. The gasp turned into a moan as his fingers lightly pinched, sending a shudder of renewed desire through her. She bent her head and sharply nipped a flat copper pap.

Jesse's eyes darkened and his teeth flashed white in his beard as he grinned. 'My God,' he groaned playfully, 'I've unleashed a wanton!' He gave a low exultant laugh and his hands cupped her hips, causing her to move convulsively against him.

Stefanie looked down at him, her eyes glowing confidently. 'Are you objecting?' she teased lightly, running her hands over his chest.

'Never! I love it,' he added in a growl, and pulled her head down to cover her lips with a quick kiss. 'I love it,' he repeated thickly, holding her eyes with a warm grey light. He brought her hand to his mouth, running the tip of his tongue over her palm. Still holding her eyes, he kissed the tip of each finger with a lingering sweetness, then lowered her hand to stroke his hip. 'I love it,' he breathed, and brought her lips down to devour his.

Once again passion controlled Stefanie. Her lips could not say, I love you, but she could express it with her body. She caressed the strong column of his neck and the velvet muscles of his chest with her lips and tongue. She felt the quickened thud of his heart as her hardened nipples brushed against him as she lowered her mouth, tasting down to the flat hardness of his stomach, and she felt him groan.

'Stefanie . . .!' Her name came hoarsely from deep within him, and with a growl he pulled her up and on to him, his hands moving her against him until passion overpowered her and she fell panting across his chest. Nuzzling soft words into the flame of hair that swept over him, Jesse turned easily with her in his arms until he was above her.

His thumbs brushed wisps of damp hair from her forehead. His smile at the surprise he saw on her face turned into a low chuckle as his scrutiny brought a fast and vivid blush to her cheeks. Suddenly shy at the strength of her uncaged sexuality, Stefanie wrapped her arms around his neck and hid her face from him.

'Do you,' she asked shakily, 'do you have any idea just what you do to me?'

'I do, sweetheart. You do it to me,' he added thickly, kissing her neck and breasts with urgent hunger. 'And it isn't over yet.' Her gasp of surprise turned into a moan of desire as his hips thrust forcefully and again she arched in need, eagerly seeking the satiating explosion of passion. At last, fulfilled, they slept wrapped in the warmth of each other's arms.

Stefanie muttered a sleepy protest when, much later, the strong arms that had been keeping her warm withdrew. 'Shhh,' Jesse hushed her gently, sliding his hands under her back and knees, lifting her easily. 'Let's go to bed, my love.'

My love! With a happy sigh, she nestled against his warmth as he climbed the stairs and laid her on the wide bed. She turned into his arms as soon as he lay down beside her, and as they tightened, she gave a contented murmur and slept again.

When next she awoke, daylight was just beginning to brighten the room. She lay still, savouring the unfamiliar feel of his body against hers, warm and hard, immensely satisfying. She allowed the delights of last night to flow through her mind, sharp and titillating pictures that caused her blood to race. Careful not to disturb him, she turned cautiously.

'I love you,' she whispered softly, reaching to touch the tousle of gold-tipped curls on the pillow beside her. She ran a loving finger along his brow, through the glossy tangle of beard to touch his lips, soft and full in sleep. He stirred under her touch and without wakening, pulled her back into his arms. With her face pressed against the comforting beat of his heart, Stefanie smiled contentedly and drifted back to sleep.

CHAPTER EIGHT

THE sound of a closing door awakened her. He's gone! she thought. She sat up in bed, pushing the heavy fall of hair from her face. The pillow beside her was empty of all but the imprint of his head. Her heart dropped with sickening suddenness before she saw the note propped up against the glass float she had found on the beach, and hastily she unfolded the paper.

Hated to wake you. Had to go—expecting a call. Come as soon as you can. J.

The brief scrawl did little to still the disquiet that had begun as soon as she realised that she was alone. She sat on the bed, hugging her knees to her chest, and gnawed nervously on a thumbnail. After the shared joys of their lovemaking last night, it was a bitter disappointment to wake up alone. Stefanie sighed. Surely he wouldn't have gone unless he had to—unless ... What if he hadn't wanted to face her this morning—could that be the reason he had left without waking her up! She stirred restlessly, striving to be reasonable. The call must be important, she thought as she kicked away the tumble of bedclothes and went to shower. Maybe it's from his publishers. But it would have been heaven to wake up with him this morning. His absence left her with a feeling of emptiness.

The hot spray cleared her head and chased away the more serious doubts. The soapy wetness of the water slid over her body that still tingled from last night's lovemaking. Surely he couldn't have been so considerate and eager to please if he didn't care, could he? she reasoned. Maybe he didn't love her, not yet, but ... Suddenly confident, she was anxious to join him.

A short time later, hair dried and loose on her shoulders, Stefanie pulled on well cut jeans, a white shirt and suede waistcoat, and added a touch of make-up to her glowing face. Feeling an urge to hurry, she grabbed a jacket and ran out the back door and along the path between the two houses. Her confidence had slipped somewhat and she was beginning to wonder how Jesse would react to her this morning. Would he be the warm and affectionate man she needed so badly—or would she see the cold, frightening side of him? Shivering in the damp greyness of the morning air, she hurried forward, anxious to put her doubts at rest.

She passed the penned birds that were quiet with food, and walked on to the porch of the house. Silently she opened the door to the kitchen. She could hear Jesse's deep voice rumbling from in the living room and realised that he must be on the phone. She crossed the kitchen floor quietly until she was able to see him. He stood with his back to her, the phone clutched in one hand, the other raking impatient fingers through his thick curls. Smiling softly at the gesture that had become so familiar to her by now, Stefanie started to go to him.

'Louisa!' She stopped abruptly at the sound of that name and the pleading tone with which it came from Jesse's lips. Without hesitation, she retreated out of sight, her heart thudding painfully. Gnawing on her thumbnail, she stayed to listen.

'Please listen, Louisa,' he was saying. 'I can't leave just now—try to understand!' Stefanie could hear his voice soften, become cajoling, and a slow numbness grew around her heart as she listened to his next words.

'Sweetheart,' he said, 'we've talked all this out before. Get started on things on your own—you can talk to the minister without me. And if you do need any help, call my mother. You know she's dying to get involved with the plans—she is the mother of the groom, after all?'

Stefanie clutched the back of the chair beside her in agony at the growing pain her love was causing her. Wanting to run, needing to hear it all, she listened as he continued talking in firm tones.

'You'll manage just fine, Louisa, and I'll be there when it really counts—in church?' He paused, then chuckled softly. 'Yes, the honeymoon has all been arranged—and no, I won't tell you where it'll be.' He added on a soft note, 'I'll tell you on your wedding day.'

Stefanie had heard more than enough. She slipped quietly out the door and dashed blindly back the way she had come. She burst through the door and stood in the middle of her kitchen, shock and despair rising in nauseating waves.

Louisa! He was going to marry Louisa! Gulping loudly, she sat down, dropping her head on to her hands. He had left her bed because he had been expecting a phone call from his fiancée. He had deceived her into thinking he was free.

I have to go, she realised with sudden clarity. Now! She stood up with a feeling of panic and moved about wildly, not knowing how to start. After a few aimless moments, she drew a deep breath to steady herself.

Calmer now, she looked around the rooms. She had few personal belongings other than her stereo and clothes. It shouldn't take long to get everything together, she decided, and methodically began to clear out her possessions. There was only one thought running through her mind. She had to be ready to leave before Jesse returned—if he did. Her breath caught on a sob and she bit hard on her lips to keep the tears at bay, afraid that if she started to cry she would not be able to stop. Resolutely, she packed the car.

Moving quickly, she checked the rooms for the last of her things. The sun caught at something on the dresser, flashing an emerald light to her searching eyes. It was the green glass float. With a surge of bitterness, she took it, turned to stand at the edge of the loft and threw it down into the living room. With more luck than aim, it hit the stone hearth and shattered into a million green shards.

Grabbing the last of her things, Stefanie ran down the stairs, out to the car, and slammed the boot on the haphazardly piled load. There was a frantic moment while she searched for the cat before she found him crouching under the car watching her every move with suspicious yellow eyes.

The relief she felt as she pulled out on to the highway was almost unnerving. She hadn't realised just how much she didn't want to see Jesse—couldn't see him. Instinct had said run, and run she had, her heart in frozen splinters. The deep sense of betrayal she felt made her thankful that she hadn't let Jesse know of her love for him. Let him think it was pure sex on her part too. At least she was spared the humiliation of having to listen to him explain that he was in love with another woman.

How could I have misjudged him so? she lamented as she drove slowly down the road. A man who calmly discusses wedding plans with his fiancée after a night in someone else's arms! It was hard to believe that he could have so little loyalty. She laughed bitterly. I know I didn't have his love, but I did think I had his friendship—and honesty! she thought.

And then with appalling clarity, she remembered how she had pleaded for his kiss—and how he had insisted that he couldn't, that he shouldn't. He hadn't hesitated out of concern for her, but out of loyalty to Louisa. He had given in to temptation because she had been deliberately enticing. Sudden tears pricked her eyes as she saw last night as it must really have been—not a time of love, but a time of lust.

A sob escaped from between her clenched teeth and her knuckles whitened as she tightened her grip on the steering wheel. Abruptly she pulled to the side of the road. There was a long hard drive ahead of her and she doubted that she had the presence of mind to make it safely. But staying meant risking being found by Jesse, and it would be doubly humiliating to be caught in the act of running away.

Shaking badly, she fought to keep tears away, her face hidden on the hands that still gripped the steering wheel. Lost in misery, she didn't hear the footsteps crunching in the gravel beside her car, and she let out a little scream of surprise at the tap on the window. It was Jim, in uniform. She rolled down the window and attempted to smile.

'Stefanie!' His own smile disappeared at the sight of her strained face. 'What's wrong—are you all right?'

She drew a long quivering breath. 'I—I'm just a little upset, that's all. I'll be okay in a minute.' Her lips moved in a poor imitation of a smile.

'You're leaving.' His quick eyes had taken in the hastily packed load on the back seat. He reached through the window and touched her shoulder. 'What's going on, Stefanie?'

'I—I . . .' She shrugged helplessly at the stutter in her voice. 'I've g-got to go.'

'You can't go anywhere in this condition.' He hesitated. 'Look, there's a coffee shop just down the road. Drive slowly—I'll follow right behind. Okay?'

He took her into the tiny restaurant and sat her in a booth with a steaming cup of coffee. Her hands trembled as she raised the cup to her lips, but the hot drink was welcome.

'Well?' he asked. 'Tell me what's going on—we're friends, aren't we?'

'We are. It's just—it's Jesse.' She lowered her eyes, playing with the spoon with nervous fingers. 'I just found out he—he doesn't care for me,' she whispered painfully. 'I—I can't stay.'

Jim touched her hand sympathetically. 'Are you sure, Stef?'

'Oh yes—I'm sure.' The harsh flatness of her voice was convincing. She raised her head and looked at him, her eyes swimming with tears. 'Thanks for the coffee, Jim. I'm okay now.' She stood up. 'I've got to go.'

Jim was frowning as he followed her out to the parking lot. 'Stefanie, I'm worried about you driving like this. Don't feel you have to go all the way today. Stop in Port Alberni for the night, will you?'

'I can't promise that, Jim.' She stopped and turned to him. 'Don't worry, I'll be careful.'

As she reached up to kiss him lightly on the cheek, his arms folded around her in a comforting embrace. 'Just see that you are,' he said gruffly. 'I don't want to pull you out from under a crushed car. Understand?'

She did. 'You're a good friend, Jim,' she said, laying

her cheek against the roughness of his uniformed chest.
'I hope I'll see you again some day.'

'I hope so too, Stef,' he said, rubbing a soothing hand
over her shoulders. 'Would you—would you like my
parents' address? If you're ever in Saskatchewan . . .'

'Would Carly mind?'

He shook his head. 'She knows how much I love her.'

'She's a lucky girl,' Stefanie said with soft sincerity.

'And Jesse's a damned fool!' Jim exploded unexpectedly. 'I've got a good mind to go and give him
hell!'

'Jim!' she said urgently. 'Promise me you won't—
don't tell him you saw me. Please!'

'All right,' he said with obvious reluctance. 'If that's
what you want, I'll keep quiet.'

'It's what I want, Jim. It wouldn't change anything
anyway.' She clung to his comforting warmth for
another moment before saying goodbye, feeling stronger
and less shaken than she had before. Tucking the paper
with his parents' address into her bag, she reached up to
kiss him lightly again. 'Thank you Jim—and good luck.'

'To you too, Stef,' he said, returning her kiss before
helping her into her car. He watched while she drove
slowly away and then returned to his own car, not once
noticing the darkly frowning man watching them from
the other side of the parking lot.

It was a long drive, tiring and increasingly torturous.
Stefanie followed the rules of the road, operating on a
purely mechanical level. It was only the overwhelming
urge to put as much distance as possible between her
and Jesse that enabled her to keep going. When the ferry
finally pulled away from the dock in Nanaimo, she
remained in her car for a long time, shaking and finally
sobbing, succumbing to the unbearable tension in both
mind and body.

The cat, already upset by the long ride, miaowed
anxiously and butted his head against her chin until she
finally raised her head. She blew her nose and dried her
eyes, then collected her handbag and jacket before
climbing to the spacious upper deck.

Many eyes followed her graceful walk through the

open area, but few saw any signs of the sadness that threatened to overwhelm her again. Already her strong defences were taking over and little of her inner turmoil showed. In the rest-room, she splashed cold water on her burning eyes, repaired her make-up and ran a brush through her hair. She went through the motions easily enough, but was unable to meet her eyes in the mirror, as though the pain she saw reflected there would be too much to accept.

Spurning food, but needing a hot drink, she bought tea at the cafeteria. Balancing it carefully, she found a quiet corner and sat sipping the tea and staring blankly at the ocean and islands slipping by until it was time to return to the car. Resolutely, she drove off the ferry and headed for the urban anonymity of Vancouver.

Pregnant. The doctor's words rang in Stefanie's ears as she stumbled from the elevator and out on to the street. Pregnant, she thought flatly. I'm pregnant. She leaned against the rough brick of the building and drew in deep steadying breaths of moisture-laden air. Slowly the dizziness passed, but the feeling of other-worldliness lingered. Too stunned to really believe, she turned and blindly walked away.

The shock of the news pounded painfully against the fragile defences she had managed to erect, and she knew she could not return to the office as she had planned to do. She needed time—time to collect her thoughts; time to adjust to this new measure of pain.

Tears stung her eyes as she walked the streets of downtown Vancouver. She wasn't going to be allowed to forget. In a few short months she would have a living memento of her fleeting interlude with love. Unless . . .

She halted the thought right there with a sharp shake of her head. Whatever had happened, whatever lay in store for her, she could not just sweep the baby from her life. She would bear and raise Jesse's child.

Hours of aimless steps brought her to the ocean's edge. She stood where the waves licked at her feet, her glazed eyes staring to the west. The wind whipped her face and tugged at her clothing, but still she stood, her

spirit flying across the waves seeking her love, her life
. . . When the dimness of the rain-blurred day deepened
into night, she turned slowly for home.

She shrugged off her wet coat, hung it on a hook
behind the door and looked around with tired eyes. It
was not a home. The walls of the tiny apartment were
bare and dingy and there was only one narrow window
that offered a dreary view of a brick wall and back
alley. The furniture was drab and shabby, cluttering the
room unattractively. It was an ugly place.

Stefanie kicked off her shoes and sat on the lumpy
couch that also served as her bed. She closed her eyes in
the wake of the exhaustion that washed over her. She
thought of all her belongings still held in storage and
felt a sudden longing to be surrounded by her own
things.

I need a home, she thought, then remembered. *We*
need a home. She frowned deeply and shook her head.
Rationally she believed and accepted the doctor's
words, but emotionally she felt no real impact. It just
wasn't real. If she hadn't required a medical for her new
job, she might not have even suspected for a few weeks
yet. It was so unexpected.

Unexpected! She gave a low, self-mocking laugh.
Most women your age know that sex without
precautions leads to pregnancy! Imagine, she thought
scornfully—an unmarried mother at twenty-six!

Stefanie stretched her tired legs out on the couch and
rubbed her flat stomach pensively with the palms of her
hands. Jesse's baby, she thought flatly. Tears pricked
the corners of her eyes. 'Poor baby,' she murmured
softly. 'Your daddy is about to be married to another
woman!'

With a sudden angry twist she stood up and began to
heave cushions against the wall. 'Damn him!' she
ground out through clenched teeth with each savage
throw. 'Damn, damn, damn him!' She kicked her shoes
clear across the room and paced angrily. It was so
unfair! It was as much his fault as it was hers, and she
felt a gloom of acid resentment.

'It would serve him right,' she stormed, 'if I showed

up at his—his wedding with a protruding stomach, sobbing through the ceremony! Or better yet, turn up with the baby squalling in my arms!' Her harsh laughter ended on a sob and she sat down shakily.

No, she realised wearily, I won't do that. She smiled sadly and clasped her hands over her stomach. I'll have his child and I'll be happy to have it. She ignored the tears that started to stream down her pale cheeks. 'It's the only part of him I'll ever have,' she whispered softly, and turned her face to the back of the couch, sobbing quietly, allowing herself tears for the first time since she had left the Island when Jesse had betrayed her trust. When he had broken her heart.

She slept somewhat better than usual that night, but awoke with the now familiar feeling of exhaustion. Most of her nights were spent tossing and turning, trying to find a comfortable spot on the couch—trying to keep sad and unwelcome thoughts at bay.

She got up reluctantly, fighting down a feeling of queasiness and showered briefly. She sat in the tiny kitchenette to apply her make-up and tried in vain to erase the dark circles under her eyes. Finally giving up, she sipped her coffee and looked around the room.

It really is ugly, she thought, certainly no place to bring a baby to. What sunlight did penetrate the grimy window only served to emphasise the dullness of the interior. Even the cat seemed to hate the place and spent most of his time with his nose pressed against the tiny crack of open window as though longing to have the freedom he was used to.

I'll start looking for something else tonight, Stefanie promised herself as she finished dressing. Even the thought of a new home was somewhat uplifting, and she knew it would be a good distraction. Glancing at the clock on the wall, she hurriedly finished her coffee and left.

She walked the short distance to her office, enjoying the first sunlight the city had had in several days. Vancouver was a beautiful city, but had a lot more rain than she was used to. But, she decided, looking around, maybe it's worth it! Everything was so green and sparkling fresh, and the air was softly perfumed. Without its shroud of cloud, she could see the forest green slopes of Grouse Mountain rising against the bright blue sky. Drawing a last deep breath of the tangy ocean air, she pushed through the doors of the office building.

The new job was very much what she had always wanted, but she found it very difficult at times to concentrate. The emotional upheaval of the last six weeks did not lend itself well to the adjustments needed in her new position. Today's tasks, fortunately, were fairly routine and she was able to keep the analytical part of her brain working while the rest puzzled ahead with tentative plans for her disrupted future. Quitting time was very welcome.

After one glance at the confusing columns in the For Rent section of the evening paper, Stefanie phoned a rental agency and told them exactly what she was looking for, demanding a list of potential places immediately. The tiny apartment felt even more confining and depressing now that she had decided to leave, and she was anxious for a new place. It proved to be an exhausting and fruitless task. Every night for the rest of the week, she hunted up addresses and viewed apartments of every sort.

Don't be so fussy, she chided herself as she left yet another unsuitable place. But she knew she couldn't live in just any place. A baby needed a bright and airy place with plenty of room for growing. A baby needed a home, and Stefanie was determined to find a place she could make into one.

In the end she found an apartment without the help of the agency. On one of her walks near English Bay, she noticed a For Rent sign in the front window of a large Victorian-style house. Intrigued by the well-kept appearance and the pretty little garden, she went to view it.

The old woman who owned the house had converted the upper floor into an apartment, complete with separate entrance. Stefanie liked it. Even bare the rooms showed a promise of warmth. There were two

big bedrooms, a living room with a tiny fireplace and a
sizeable kitchen with a breakfast nook overlooking the
garden. Within minutes, Stefanie had made up her
mind.

'I'll take it,' she said, then stopped. 'That is—if you
don't mind children? I—I'm pregnant. And I'm not
married.' She touched her stomach with an unconscious
gesture.

The old woman studied her for a shrewd moment,
then shrugged. 'Only one thing concerns me—can you
pay the rent?'

A short time later Stefanie was back in the street with
the key to her new home. She hurried back to her
apartment, exhausted after the long week of searching.

She was glad to fall into bed that night—at least for a
while. In spite of her physical fatigue, her mind just
wouldn't stop. There were questions she should have
been asking herself already. If she planned on keeping
the baby—and she did—then she needed some answers.
Even now she was beginning to see some of the many
problems she would face as a single parent.

How long could she keep working? And what about
afterwards, when the baby was born—would she be
ready to leave it after the relatively short time allowed
for maternity leave? If so, who was going to look after
it? Someone warm and loving, of course—but would it
be easy to find someone she would be willing to leave
her newborn child with?

Stefanie sighed and rolled over, giving her pillow a
restless punch. Each question just seemed to give rise to
more questions. And it was answers she needed. Giving
up on sleep, she went into the kitchenette to make
herself a warm drink. Obviously the time had come for
some serious thinking.

She sat in the armchair, sipping a cup of hot
chocolate. With a sigh of deep weariness that went far
beyond the physical, she closed her eyes and leaned her
head against the back of the chair. Oh, Jesse, she
thought with a prick of tears. I need you. Why couldn't
you love me?

She sat up abruptly and rubbed her eyes dry, pushing

the feeling of loss and hurt deep inside. There was no time now for futile emotions and regrets. There were things to be done, practical things. Soon there would be a new life depending on her, a dependency that was going to last for a long time, and she wanted to be prepared.

What bothered her most at the moment was the idea of leaving the baby when she had to return to work. How was it going to feel leaving her tiny infant in someone else's arms when her leave was up? She would miss the baby's first smiles, and coos, its rapt discovery of itself and, later, of her. That first year was a time of incredible growth and she would have to miss most of it. She shook her head, not liking the idea at all. Maybe it was because she had lost her own mother at such an early age.

She couldn't remember her mother—not her face or voice, but she had never forgotten her presence. She had memories of lullabys and gentle laughter, of stories at bedtime and cool fingers soothing her fevered brow. They were more feelings than memories, feelings of comfort and love. Stefanie sighed. If only there was some way she could stay at home with her child—if only for a few months!

Suddenly her eyes flew open and she sat up, staring straight ahead. Stephen Foster. Of course! Excited now, she reached for the telephone. 'Operator?' she asked impatiently. 'I'd like Directory Assistance in Winnipeg, please.'

Twenty minutes later she replaced the receiver, her mood elevated. Mr Foster had first assured her that, indeed, he did not mind being phoned at home, and in dry lawyer tones went on to explain that financially she was quite secure. Stefanie sat back in her chair with a deep sigh of relief.

Her father had left her a considerable amount of money. Most of it, however, came from various insurance policies paid up after his untimely death when the small plane in which he was flying crashed shortly after take-off from a remote northern community. To Stefanie, in her intense grief, the money had been

tainted, and she had told the lawyers handling her
father's estate, in no uncertain terms, that she wanted
none of it. But now, realising that the money would
ultimately benefit the grandchild he would never know,
she felt no qualms about using it. Her father would
want it that way—so her child could be with her, as she
had been with him.

Stefanie turned out the lights and climbed back into
bed, amazed at what an effective sedative good financial
news could be. 'Thanks, Dad,' she whispered, curled up
and went to sleep. Tonight there were no visions of
gold-tipped curls and warm grey eyes to haunt her
sleep.

She left her job the next day. It was not an easy
move for her to make, but in the circumstances, she felt
it was the best one. She would be better prepared to
continue her career in a year or so.

The rest of the week, she spent painting and moving
into her new apartment. When it was finally finished,
she stood in the middle of the living room, and looked
around with satisfaction.

The floor in front of the tiny hearth was covered with
an area rug that looked like a splash of rich cream on
the golden glow of the freshly polished oak floor. The
couch, an overstuffed burgundy print, was arranged to
face the fireplace and there was a brass-trimmed glass
coffee table immediately in front. There were two
comfortable chairs and cushions in a complementary
blend of colours.

'Well, Pete,' she said, 'this is it—home again!' But the
words sounded forced. Nice as it looked, something was
missing, and that something, she knew, came from
within her. In her present state, she was just going
through the motions of making a home. The hollowness
she felt inside was reflected in the apartment, and no
amount of decorating would ever add that warm glow
needed to make the apartment complete.

Stefanie sighed and sat down. Now that the moving
was done she suddenly realised just how much time she
was going to have on her hands. In the fall she could
enrol in a computer course at the University to fill in

the time, but that left the whole summer with little to do but think ...

She rubbed her hand across tired eyes. Were Jesse and Louisa already married? Were they living in Vancouver where there would always be a chance she might run into them? She remembered the pain she had felt when she had seen the two of them together on the beach that morning on the island—how much more painful it would be to see them together now! She bit her lip hard to keep the tears from falling. She was through with crying. Impulsively, she ran downstairs to invite her landlady up for tea. She felt a desperate need for company.

'I know it's none of my business,' the old woman said as she was leaving, 'but I think you'd better take it easy now that all the moving is done.' She waved a precautionary finger at Stefanie. 'Growing babies takes a lot of energy, and you don't look like you've got much to spare.' With a wave of her hand, she trotted briskly down the stairs and disappeared into her rooms.

She's right, Stefanie thought later as she peered into the bathroom mirror. She picked up a strand of dry hair and wrinkled her nose in disgust. Look at me— scrawny and haggard! And I thought pregnant women were supposed to blossom!

Underlying the hollow cheeks and shadowed eyes was a fragile look of a haunting sadness. She had pushed all thought of Jesse deep inside, trying to look ahead stoically. But the smouldering yearnings for a tall man with gold-tipped curls and flashing grey eyes were taking their toll.

Stefanie turned away from the mirror fully determined to rest. She sat on the edge of her bed willing herself to relax, to stretch out on the bedspread and give her body the rest it craved. She couldn't. She felt a surge of the edginess that plagued her so often now, and jumped up. Walking provided the only relief other than sleeping. If she couldn't do one, she'd do the other. She grabbed a light sweater from the closet and left the house.

The rent Mrs Gardner charged for her place was relatively low when one considered the advantages of the location. Not only did the tenant get four large and charming rooms and use of the pretty yard, but easy access to English Bay and Stanley Park as well.

English Bay was an attractive curve of sandy beach that edged the most populous district of the city. Hundreds of high-rise apartment buildings clustered its perimeter and overlooked the busy waters. Also offered to view was the huge and naturally forested Stanley Park, a haven in the bustling city. It offered residents and tourists alike a zoo, aquarium, golf links ... and, best of all, Stefanie had come to realise on one of her many walks along woody paths, a chance to disappear from the city.

Within minutes of leaving, she was in the park. Her rapid strides slowed as soon as she came in sight of the relaxing green lawns, gigantic spreading trees and colourful flower gardens. Choosing an empty bench near the Lost Lagoon, she sat quietly, relishing the heat of the June sun on her shoulders.

The lagoon was a busy place. Swans, ducks and geese swam across the water noisily encouraging their young broods to keep up. Children squatted along the shore throwing fistfuls of dry bread to the eager birds. It was a summer Sunday in the park, a good place to be distracted from personal miseries.

Or so she thought. She was diverted from her study of the Lagoon by a small clucking noise and turned to see a big Canada Goose watching her with shiny black eyes. With a rush the memory of the first day she had really met Jesse came back to her. He had been kneeling by the pen, talking about a bird much like this one, his eyes filled with soft sympathy for the wild bird's plight. She could almost hear him as he told her in quiet informative tones of the breeding habits of the Canada Goose—lifelong and loyal.

Stefanie jumped up with a suddenness that sent the bird squawking for the water. How long is this going to go on? she asked herself in despair. The man is a liar and a cheat—forget him!

She raced over the grounds at a furious pace, as though she could outrun the memories and the pain.

That part of her life was over, and the sooner she could forget about it, the better it would be for her and the baby.

The baby! A sharp stabbing pain in her side brought her to a hasty stop, her hands clutching her stomach. It was just a stitch, she realised thankfully after a minute, but she had seen in that short time just how utterly dependent her child was on her—now. Not just in a few months' time, but now, at this very moment. Unless she started to take care of herself by eating and sleeping properly, the growing child would be deprived as surely as if she withheld proper care after birth.

It was a sobering thought. For the first time, Stefanie's emotions made the connection with her pregnancy. She sat down abruptly under a spreading tree and brought her knees up to hug them against her stomach.

She knew then just how much she wanted this baby, her baby and Jesse's, conceived out of her love for him. No matter what difficulties lay in store for her, the baby was already an important part of her life. The first warm trickles of love for her unborn child stirred her frozen heart, and a welcome peace descended upon her as she sat alone on the lush green grass.

Stefanie sat for a long time before she finally moved on. She walked slowly this time, a soft smile giving light to her tired face. Unconsciously, her hands would reach down to touch her stomach as if to reassure the tiny life in her womb of its welcome.

Her wandering took her to the zoo, still brimming with the afternoon's visitors. She found her eyes drawn more and more to the children. One tiny girl in a bright yellow sundress trotted unsteadily away from her mother, raising chubby arms high in the air. She squinted her eyes at the sun and squealed in sheer delight. Stefanie met the young mother's eyes and they shared a smile at the sweetness of the happy child.

It's going to be all right, she thought with wary sureness. The sadness was still there, but somehow it no longer felt debilitating. With a strong feeling of relief, she turned to go home.

She pampered and petted herself over the next few days. There was no alarm clock nagging at her to get up in the mornings and she slept late. She was careful to eat proper meals, and soon found herself looking forward to meals again. With lots of rest and relaxation, she slowly began to fill out, and her face lost the gaunt and hollow-eyed look of heartbreak.

'You're looking much better,' the landlady said with approval one morning as they shared the back yard.

'I feel better,' Stefanie murmured sleepily. She was lying on a blanket wearing a wispy green bikini, content to soak up the sun. She stretched and yawned hugely. 'Now, if only I could keep awake!'

'If you're going to sleep, come out of the sun,' the old woman cautioned. 'You'll burn to a crisp with that fair skin!'

Smiling at the other woman's concern, Stefanie fastened the back strap of the bikini top and moved to a lounge chair under the shade of a big maple tree. 'It's not burning that worries me—it's freckles.' She wrinkled her nose. 'I hate freckles!' Unbidden came the memory of Jesse in her bedroom on the Island, waking her with soft sensuality, his long finger tracing the pattern of freckles on her nose. She blinked rapidly to stop the tears before they could fall, and mumbling an excuse to Mrs Gardner, ran upstairs. Her pillow was damp with sadness before she finally drifted into a troubled sleep.

Later that day, unable to relax for the first time in days, Stefanie wandered through the rooms of the apartment. They were looking good, and she made a note of the corners that could use a plant or two to finish them off. She found herself suddenly imagining that she was making a home not only for her and the baby, but for Jesse as well. Try as she might, she could not erase the big vibrant man from her heart. She missed him. In those few short weeks on the Island, he had become her best friend as well as her lover and the father of her child. She missed him—and he had deceived her . . .

Battling the new surge of pain, Stefanie leaned in the

doorway of the baby's room. It hadn't been touched except for a coat of soft white paint, and she studied the bareness thoughtfully. It might be early, but why not decorate it now, when her need for action was the greatest? It would fill in some of the space in the empty stretch of days that lay before her.

The task was enjoyable. She took her time with the room, using the pleasurable experience to fight the depression that still hovered over her like a dark menace. By the time she was finished, it was time for her second trip to the doctor.

The visit was reassuring. Stefanie was heartily relieved to learn that the baby hadn't been harmed by her earlier depression and run-down condition. Slowly her unborn child had come to mean salvation. In order to take care of the baby, she was forced to take care of herself—it was a lifeline to sanity. If anything happened to the baby ... Stefanie clenched her hands until the knuckles were white. Nothing would happen.

Arriving home after the successful visit to the doctor, she felt an urge to go out. She enjoyed a solitary life—to a point. She sighed. There was just no one in Vancouver to whom she could turn for companionship. With a shrug, she decided to treat herself to a good restaurant meal. So what if she would be alone? Determined to make the best of it, she showered and dressed carefully.

She looked vitally alive and beautiful as she left her apartment. She wore a green and gold cotton skirt with an ivory camisole tucked into the gathered waistband. The skirt's fit was rather snug and her breasts, fuller in pregnancy, gave a saucy push against the fine material of the camisole, so she slipped into a short cotton jacket overall. Her hair shimmered on her shoulders radiating firelights from the late sun, and her eyes gleamed in the honey tan of her face, echoing the warm smile on her soft lips. Tonight she felt good.

Tall and confident, she entered the restaurant, dazzled the head waiter with a smile and sweetly commanded a table in a secluded corner. Her waiter and the wine steward were equally impressed with her

warm manner and gave faultless service. Three delicious
courses and a half bottle of wine later, Stefanie sat back
with a good cup of coffee. The meal had bordered on
excellence, and when she paid the bill, she added a
generous tip. Giving the waiter a cheeky wink, she
walked cheerfully back on to the street.

It was still light although the shadows were long and
the air was taking on a night time softness. Stefanie
wanted to hang on to the good feeling she had tonight,
and had no desire to return to her empty rooms and the
memories that lay waiting to taunt her with vivid
recollections of a love that couldn't be. She felt a strong
urge for company and if there was no one to turn to,
she could at least share the remainder of the evening
with other aimless souls along the beach at English Bay.

She sat for a while, looking over the water at the
cargo ships, sailboats and the occasional canoes on the
bay. There was still plenty of activity on the beach as
well, but even as she watched, people began to leave.
Tired parents coaxed their fractious children to pack
away the pails and shovels for another day. Elderly
people got up stiffly, rolling down pants legs and shirt-
sleeves before leaving.

As it grew later, young people began to drift in. The
youngest came in mixed groups, boisterous with
freedom. Older ones came in pairs, giddy with young
love, one minute tearing up the sand in laughing
pursuit, the next wrapping their arms around each
other, aware of no one else.

Stefanie stood up, sighing slightly. I wish I'd had a
chance to do all that as a teenager, she thought
wistfully, then shrugged. Would it have made any
difference to what she was feeling now? She wandered
aimlessly along the beach to the water's edge. Reaching
down, she unfastened the tiny buckles on her sandals
and continued to walk ankle-deep in the frothy water.

It made her think of other times, on another beach
with a tall man walking beside her carefully drawing her
attention to the wonders of ocean life. She could see
him vividly, standing with bearded chin outthrust, an
offshore breeze ruffling his gold-tipped curls.

Stefanie splashed along slowly, sandals dangling from one hand as she struggled to keep her mind on the pleasant memories she had of her time with Jesse. Such a short time, an infinitely sweet time, until ... No! She shook her head. She wouldn't think about it. Her lips tightened and she rubbed the tears from her eyes as she walked a little faster watching the water splash against her smooth brown calves.

She wasn't sure when she first realised that someone was watching her, following her. She slowly became aware of an intrusion on her solitude. She kept glancing over her shoulder, trying to find the cause of her unease, but there was no one to be seen in the lengthening twilight. Cautious now, she turned back in the direction she had come. As beautiful a spot as it was, she was still in the middle of a large city and a lonely stretch of beach was not a safe place for a woman to be after dark.

She saw him suddenly and without real surprise, a featureless shadow detaching itself from the surrounding darkness. Slowly, so that it was barely perceptible, she quickened her steps, desperately wanting to be on the other side of him before their paths intercepted. In that direction lay the more public part of the beach and protection from the threat coming towards her with relentless strides.

Suddenly panic-stricken, Stefanie bolted. She ran like a deer with hounds at heel, her eyes wide with terror, the wind whipping a soundless scream from her lips. She heard footsteps behind her pounding louder than the surf, coming closer and closer ... a hard and heavy hand closed over her shoulder, a ragged panting sounded harsh in her ear.

'Running again?' The words were ground out with savage mockery.

With a quick twist, she flung off the restraining hand. She stood incredulous, staring with eyes round with lingering horror. 'You!' She drew a deep shuddering breath and stared past the hard jut of square jaw into eyes as cold and grey as winter seas. 'You—you shaved,' she said in a dazed whisper, and slowly sank to the damp sand, sheltered by a fuzzy blanket of darkness.

Consciousness required too much effort. Stefanie ignored the voice that called her name urgently, a voice that must belong to a dream because she couldn't be hearing it. She was vaguely aware of strong arms folding around her and lifting her easily. The thudding heart and warm male smell reminded her of another time and place. With a tiny sound, she rubbed her cheek against the hard chest. 'Jesse,' she whispered softly, and returned to that black and soundless void.

When she came around completely, she was lying on her own bed. 'Wha...?' She shook her head in confusion and tried to sit up.

'Lie still, girl!' she was commanded in firm tones. Obeying more because of dizziness than anything else, Stefanie turned to Mrs Gardner.

'Where is he?' She knew it hadn't been a dream.

'I sent him to the kitchen to make you a cup of tea,' the landlady answered promptly. The old woman's eyes sparkled with avid curiosity. 'Is he...?'

Stefanie closed her eyes and nodded briefly. As the last of the dizziness faded and clarity returned, her eyes flew open and she asked urgently, 'Did you say anything—about the baby?'

'Not a word,' she was assured. 'Didn't reckon it was my place. I was in the garden when he walked up with you in his arms—he said he got the address from your bag after you fainted. What happened?'

Stefanie shrugged. 'I was—startled, I guess. I feel fine now.' It was true. She sat up, swinging her legs over the edge of the bed to prove it.

'Take it easy,' Mrs Gardner cautioned. 'There's no hurry for you to get up.'

'Oh yes, there is!' Stefanie insisted, standing up slowly. She let out a deep breath—the room stayed still.

Mrs Gardner studied her closely for a moment. 'Well, if you're sure everything is all right, I'll go downstairs. Looks like you two have some talking to do!'

Stefanie merely smiled as the old woman left. She took a quick look to see that the door to the baby's room was closed—he mustn't see that! Drawing another deep breath in a vain attempt to steady her nerves, she walked quietly to the kitchen.

He was standing with his back to her, staring out the window to the dark garden below. From behind he looked much like he had on the Island, except that he wore well tailored grey slacks instead of worn jeans. A cream-coloured cotton shirt hugged his shoulders and he had turned the cuffs up over strong brown forearms. She saw that the gold-tipped curls had been cut and his hair neatly styled. And his beard had gone, she remembered with a pang of regret as he turned to take the boiling kettle from the stove.

He started a bit when he saw her leaning casually against the door frame. His eyes swept over her quickly, lifting to meet hers with a blaze that died before it really started. He turned slightly and waved his hand in the air. 'I was going to make tea—where is it?'

'I'll get it,' Stefanie said with studied calmness. 'Sit down.'

'You're the one who should be sitting down—passing out like that!'

'What did you expect, coming at me like a drug-crazed mugger!' She glared at him. 'You scared the hell out of me!'

Jesse leaned back against the counter and calmly crossed his arms over his wide chest. 'Good. You shouldn't have been wandering alone down there at that time of the night.'

'Maybe I didn't plan on being alone for long,' she taunted. 'Maybe I was meeting somebody.'

'Then I should have waited and let him carry you back,' he returned smoothly. 'You're somewhat heavier than—er—the last time I carried you.'

Stefanie swung around busily setting cups on a tray to hide the flush that stained her cheeks. She remembered only too well the time he was referring to.

'Fat and happy,' he continued with a strong undertone of bitterness. 'That's exactly how you looked tonight walking on the beach.'

'Spying on me?' she asked with a sharp edge of

sarcasm which he ignored. She spared a moment to glance at her stomach. It was rounder and softer, yes, but she was not obviously pregnant. Relieved that he was unlikely to guess that she was carrying his child, she picked up the tray and started towards the kitchen door.

'If you plan on staying for tea,' she said in a cold and polite voice, 'may I suggest the living room? It's so much more comfortable.'

'Give me that,' he said roughly, and took the tray from her. He followed her down the hall and set the tray on the coffee table. 'Very nice,' he said after a quick look around. 'All this belongs to you?'

So, Stefanie sighed to herself, we're going to make polite conversation, are we? She nodded. 'I had it shipped in from Winnipeg.' She sat down on the couch and indicated that he should take one of the chairs. To her relief, he did. Even at that distance, he was too close for her fragile peace of mind.

They sat in silence while she poured the tea. 'So— how is Aggie?' she asked with a forced brightness. Anything to break the heavy silence.

'Aggie is fine—although she would have appreciated hearing from you. She actually grew quite fond of you.' His tone strongly implied that he couldn't understand it.

Stefanie shrugged off the twinge of guilt his words stirred. 'And how have you been?' How was your wedding, was what she wanted to ask in a carefree, I couldn't-care-less kind of voice, but there was no way she could manage that much control.

'Me?' he said. 'Oh, fine, just fine.' His words were heavy with sarcasm. Stefanie's eyes flew to his face, but it was impassive.

She sighed and took a sip of tea before plunging on, determined to remain calm and polite in spite of his brooding silences. 'What is it that brings you here?'

'If memory serves me correct,' he said in the same heavy tone, 'you passed out on the beach, and like a gentleman, I carried you home.'

'Thanks very much,' Stefanie said dryly. 'I meant, what were you doing on the beach?'

'Taking a walk,' he replied shortly with a sardonic twist to his lips.

She rolled her eyes up in disgust. He was being deliberately infuriating! What game was he playing? The whole thing tonight was just too much of a coincidence to be accidental. Had he been looking for her? Why?

She stole a look at him. He sat there staring moodily at the empty hearth, looking much more handsome and urbane than he had on the Island. Almost like a stranger, she thought with a sharp ache. Was this the real Jesse—this man with the mocking twist to his lips and the cruel light in his eyes? Had the big gentle man she had loved on the Island been just an illusion of time and place?

Stefanie rubbed a hand over the back of her neck. The tension was beginning to get to her, and she felt a soul-deep weariness descend on her. *Just when I thought I was going to be all right,* she thought bitterly. *Why did he have to show up now?* She gnawed her thumbnail in rising desperation. *I don't need this* she thought. Knowing tears weren't far away, she stood up suddenly.

'I think you'd better go, Jesse,' she said, unable to hide the bitterness she felt. 'I—I don't want you here.' She turned swiftly and went to stand by the window. Her nerves were stretched too tautly for her to be able to play any more games with him. The sooner he left, the sooner she could get on with her own life. Her empty life.

She heard him get up and bit her lip to keep from calling out to him. He didn't leave. She felt him come up behind her, felt his strong hands close painfully over her shoulders. She trembled at his touch and for an instant ached to lean against him and feel his arms close around her.

'And why don't you want me here?' His voice was harsh in her ear. 'Guilty conscience, Stefanie?'

She shrugged off his hands and whirled around, eyes glazing. 'Guilty? Me? I'm not the one who . . .' Aghast, she stopped. She had to let him think she left because

she didn't want him. It was the only way she could
salvage what was left of her pride.

'Not the one who what, Stefanie?' His voice was quiet
and demanding.

Stefanie stood resolute, head held high and proudly
stubborn.

Jesse sighed and turned away from her, rubbing his
forehead in a curious gesture. His next question came as
a complete surprise. 'Did you know Jim got married
last week?'

She shook her head in bewilderment. 'Jim?' she
repeated blankly. What did he have to do with all this?

'Yes, Jim,' Jesse said harshly. 'The man you ran to—
remember?'

'I didn't run to anybody!' Her voice rose with puzzled
indignation. 'Jim bought me a cup of coffee to—to say
goodbye, that's all!'

Jesse's lips curled in a sneer. 'Wasn't a parking lot a
little public for such a protracted—goodbye?'

'Y-you were there!' Stefanie's face whitened. How
close he had been to catching up with her!

'I saw it all,' he said bitterly. 'I was trying to find
you—to find out why you were leaving like that. I
thought maybe you'd misunderstood something I'd
said.' He laughed harshly. 'I was really off track, wasn't
I?' His words were cruel. 'Once you'd—used me to get
over your sexual hangups, you couldn't get out fast
enough!'

Stefanie threw up her hands. 'I used you!' Her voice
almost squeaked with rage. 'Just what in the hell did
you expect me to do—hang around and wait for an
invitation to the wedding?' She clenched her fists at her
sides, strongly tempted to hit him.

'What wedding?' Jesse was alert, the anger and scorn
gone from his face.

'What wedding?' she mimicked sarcastically. 'The
wedding you were so carefully planning over the phone
with Louisa—that wedding. Remember now?'

'Yes,' he said succinctly, 'I remember.'

'I thought you would,' she said with a saccharine
smile. 'I thought you'd forgotten—again.'

'So I had.' Jesse's voice was nonchalant as he studied her closely.

'Poor, poor Louisa,' Stefanie sneered, hanging on to her anger to keep the tears at bay. 'Doesn't she get tired of these—lapses in your memory?'

Jesse shrugged. 'Actually, I don't think she even notices.' His voice took on a lighter tone, and he stared at her with an unnerving closeness.

He's wearing me down, Stefanie thought. The feeling of panic caused her to miss his next words—almost.

Startled, she looked at him openly for the first time that night. 'Wh-what did you say?'

His eyes held hers as he came closer. 'I said,' he repeated, 'why don't you ask her—when she gets back from her honeymoon?'

'Her—her honeymoon?' Stefanie stammered, looking helplessly into his eyes, so warm now, so close . . .

'Yes, Stefanie,' he said, lifting a hand to her face and rubbing a finger over her parted lips. 'Her honeymoon— and Jarred's. He's my younger brother. He was working north of Edmonton and couldn't get away until just before the wedding. And so, like the good big brother I am, I promised to help Louisa with the arrangements.'

Stefanie swallowed painfully, mesmerised by the stroking finger. 'So Louisa is . . .' She stopped. As her lips formed the words they pressed against his finger like tiny kisses.

'My sister-in-law,' he finished for her. 'Not my fiancée, Stefanie, not my wife—just a sweet girl who married my brother.' His hands came down to rest on her shoulders.

'Aggie didn't seem to think she was so sweet,' Stefanie said stubbornly. It was hard to let go of the idea that he was involved with Louisa. So many times in the last weeks she had pictured them together, married, loving . . .

'Aggie, I think, is inclined to liken her to Wanda.' His eyes darkened. 'They really aren't alike at all, aside from their looks.'

Stefanie remembered those blonde and curvaceous looks. 'But I saw you—together on the beach. You kissed her.' The words were flat. Too many times had that memory come back to hurt her.

'How did I kiss her, Stefanie?' he asked gently. 'Was it like this?' His lips touched hers briefly. 'Or this?' His voice was low and caressing as his mouth descended again, this time covering her quivering lips with searing heat. It was too brief. He raised his head and smiled down at her. 'Well? Did I kiss her like that?' He held her close to him.

Stefanie licked her lips nervously. 'I—er—no.' She shook her head and sighed tremulously. 'I—it wasn't like that.' Hope was slowly awakening.

'And never has been. I've known Louisa since she was eight years old, Stefanie. She's always been my kid sister. Can you understand that?' His eyes were serious.

She could only nod. She looked at him, her eyes round with uncertainty. His lips were curved in a soft smile and his eyes seemed to caress her face as he watched her. He was waiting.

Stefanie drew a deep breath and began to talk. 'I—I came over th-that morning,' she said, staring at his unfamiliar jaw. 'You were on the phone, so I came in quietly. I—I heard you talking about the wedding, the honeymoon—and Aggie had seemed to think you and Louisa were involved, a-and I'd seen her at your place one morning ... Oh, Jesse,' she said, looking at him earnestly, 'it sounded like you were planning your own wedding!' Her eyes clouded in memory. 'I—I felt so awful, Jesse, I had to go. I'm sorry,' she ended on a whisper, and dropped her eyes.

Jesse cupped the sides of her face, his thumbs pushing the hair back from her temples. 'I waited for you that morning—I thought you'd never come. Finally I went to roust you out of bed—although I planned on taking my time about it.' He smiled gently at her sudden blush. 'When I got there, I found the door locked, your car gone ... I finally realised that you'd packed up and gone.' With a quick movement he folded her into his arms and held her close.

'I got in somehow—there wasn't even a note. Nothing. Just your crystal ball smashed against the fireplace,' he said with a bleak voice. 'I knew that you couldn't have been gone long, so I went after you. Only to find you with Jim.' His voice hardened. 'Tell me there was nothing between you, Stefanie.'

'Nothing but friendship,' she said readily. 'He knew I was—was upset, and comforted me, that's all.' Hope was fully alert now. She pressed her cheek closer to the warmth of his chest. She felt him let out a shaky sigh.

'Do you know how long I've been hanging around English Bay and the park?' he murmured raggedly against her hair. 'I knew you wanted to live around here—and I had no other way of finding you. It was my only hope—that some day I'd get lucky and see you.'

Stefanie leaned back in his arms and looked at him. 'So why did you chase me?'

Jesse sighed and shrugged lightly. 'I guess I'd been building up this picture of finding you—just like a writer would do,' he added. 'You'd be walking along looking sad and lonely—looking as miserable as I felt. Instead,' he said with a hint of bitterness, 'you looked even better than you had on the Island, wading through the water looking so content and breaking into dreamy little smiles.' He shook his head. 'It made me angry and I began to realise that you'd run away because it was the easiest way to break off an unwanted relationship.'

'Oh, no, Jesse—it was never that way. You must believe me!' She was desperate that there be no more misunderstandings. For the first time in many weeks, she had begun to hope again.

'I know that now, Stefanie,' he reassured her. 'And I'm sorry I scared you like that. If it's any consolation, you scared the hell out of me too, with that blackout!'

She parted her lips to tell him of the real reason behind her faint, but hesitated. He had to know about the baby, and soon, but there was still so much to be said. Maybe the next little while should belong to just the two of them. She dropped her head on his shoulder with a little sigh.

'I missed you so much, Jesse,' she whispered, and felt his arms tighten. 'It was hard for me to believe that I'd been so wrong about you—but what I'd overheard

seemed so—so very real. I felt horribly betrayed, Jesse.'
She ran her arms around his back and pulled him close
to her. 'I've been so very unhappy,' she confessed softly,
a sigh of sadness echoing in her voice.

'And I thought you were with Jim,' Jesse admitted. 'I
would have looked for you sooner if it wasn't for that,'
he added. 'It was only last month that Tom mentioned
that he'd received a wedding invitation from Jim—and
then told me like I was some kind of fool that it wasn't
you he was marrying!' He rubbed his chin against the
satiny softness of her hair.

'We let things happen too fast, Stefanie. If I'd said all
I should have said—wanted to say—on that beautiful
night when we made love, we would have been spared
so much of this—this anguish.' The hardness of pain
was in his voice.

Stefanie knew then that his suffering had equalled her
own. She raised her head and smiled into his eyes,
confident now, and knowing. 'What was it you should
have said?' she whispered.

His eyes held hers, sincerity and promise in their
depths. 'That I love you and want to marry you.' The
words were softly impassioned.

Stefanie's breath caught and her face lit with her wide
and beautiful smile. She gasped as the grey eyes blazed
into hers and his hands slid from her waist to her hips,
pulling her pliant body to his.

'Kiss me,' he commanded in a husky whisper, and
she complied with parted lips, anxious to feel his love,
to give him hers. Separation had not dampened the fire
that flamed between them, and when they drew apart
they were breathless and smiling with happy excitement.

'Will you?' he asked.

Stefanie blinked. 'Will I what?'

'Marry me,' he said, holding her against him as if he
would never let her go.

Stefanie wound her arms around his neck, her eyes
glowing with happiness. 'On one condition,' she said
softly.

His body tensed. 'Anything,' he promised in a
strained voice.

'Grow your beard back,' she whispered, drawing a finger along the hard line of his jaw.

'You've got it.' He relaxed with a chuckle. 'Anything else?'

'Nope.' She dimpled. 'Consider yourself caught!'

'Oh, I'm caught all right,' he said softly looking deep into her eyes. 'Hook, line and sinker. I think you managed to do that the first time I saw you—standing on the beach dripping wet and highly indignant.' He smiled at her. 'You touched something in me, Stefanie—right away. And then let me think you were too young to be taken seriously!'

'In a lot of ways I was,' she admitted. 'If you'd known just how old I was . . .' She shrugged and shook her head. 'I might have run then and there—although I doubt if I would ever have had much peace of mind after that. You—you touched something in me too, Jesse,' she said softly. 'Something beautiful and trusting.'

His mouth lowered as she raised her face to his. His lips touched hers with an aching tenderness that spoke of a love far beyond the passion they aroused in each other, a kiss so sweet, Stefanie felt tears of happiness well in her eyes.

'Stefanie—oh, my love,' Jesse cried softly, burying his face in her soft warm neck. 'I want you—I need you so badly.' Each word was like a torch on the skin of her throat.

Stefanie grasped his head and pulled it up. Her soft mouth reached to touch his face, caressing his jaw, his cheeks, his eyes and brow. Tears of joy trembled in her vivid eyes. 'I love you, Jesse,' she said at last, and his mouth closed over hers, tasting the tender words.

It was enough for a while to stand in the healing shelter of each other's arms, exchanging murmured words of love and promises for a bright future. They kissed and caressed softly, restoring the trust that had been so badly shattered, gathering strength and renewing what they had so fleetingly grasped on the Island.

Jesse's hands moved over her body, becoming more

and more urgent. He slid his hands under the loose jacket she wore and with a quick movement removed it and let it drop to the floor. His mouth moved over face as he stroked with trembling fingers across her breasts that pushed taut and aching with growing desire against the fine material of the camisole.

'Jesse!' Stefanie's voice came in a gasp and she pushed half-heartedly at his shoulders. 'I—I think we'd better move.' She swallowed convulsively as his hands continued their seductive caresses. 'A-away from the window, I mean.'

Without a word, Jesse swooped her up into his arms and carried her to the bedroom. He stood her in the middle of the floor, claiming her lips in an explosive touch. He rubbed his palms over her breasts, then reached impatiently to fumble at the tiny pearl buttons.

Understanding his urgency and weakened with the shock waves of her own desire, Stefanie stepped back to unfasten the top herself. She lingered over each button with a deliberate slowness that inflamed him. Her nipples grew hard under his hungry gaze, anticipating the touch of his teasing mouth. Still he watched, even as the silky material fell unheeded to the floor.

She wetted her lips with the tip of her tongue. Slowly her hands went behind her back, thrusting her full breasts into perfect outline with the movement. With nimble fingers she unfastened the zipper of her skirt and let it slide over her hips to join the camisole on the floor. Jesse's eyes burned with love and passion, but he stood still, his very stance hypnotising, until, slowly and sensuously, she removed the tiny scrap of lace from her hips.

'My love,' he said huskily. 'My beautiful love.' His fingers stroked the dusky rose nipples with feather lightness. 'Undress me,' he commanded hoarsely.

Stefanie obeyed. Her breath quickened as each unfastened button revealed more of the chest that had browned under the summer sun. She slid her hands, cool on his heated flesh, up over his stomach to his chest and played with the hard muscles of his shoulders before pulling the shirt off and letting it fall to the floor. She came closer and planted biting kisses on his body while her fingers fumbled hesitatingly with his belt buckle.

With a groan of impatience, Jesse finished the task himself with quick barely controlled motions. At last there was no barrier to their seeking hands, and they melted together with a kiss that sealed their love and stormed their desire. Slowly they sank on to the cool satin bedspread and stretched out full length, stroking and kissing eagerly, delighting in the sight and feel of each other as they murmured words of love and passion.

As their desires grew, the touches became more demanding and urgent, as though the lovemaking was a final release from the pain and tensions they had unwittingly caused each other. There was nothing Jesse did with his hands and mouth that Stefanie did not answer passionately.

She moaned in abandon as his lips blazed a torturous trail over her sensitised skin. He played at her breasts with lips and tongue until she could stand it no longer. Without stopping his mouth kissed and dallied over her stomach to caress her hips and thighs, each touch adding to her intense longing.

'Jesse!' Her gasp of desire turned into a low moan as his tongue lingered erotically on her tender flesh. 'Please, Jesse—now!' she whispered in a frenzy. She groaned as his leg thrust between hers and at last their desires joined in a molten clash. They moved in unison, upward and outward with a passion that finally blazed with a white-hot heat that seared and then satiated.

They lay entwined for a long time afterwards, apart too long to want the separation of sleep. They talked and laughed softly, savouring the joy of being together again, for ever and always.

'When do you want to get married?' Jesse asked lazily, stroking her hair as she lay with her head on his shoulder.

Stefanie was silent. She had to tell him about the baby. It couldn't wait any longer. Without giving him

the answer he waited for, she rolled on to her back,
searching for a way to tell him.

'Jesse . . .' She hesitated. Then, with determination,
she reached for his hand and drew it down to the soft
roundness of her stomach. At that moment their baby
began to stir with soft fluttery movements that felt
like tiny bubbles bursting under her skin. She pressed
the palm of his hand flat against the motion.

'Jesse,' she started again, and drew a deep breath.
'I—we—are going to have a baby.' The words came out
in a rush. 'I'm pregnant.' There—it had been said. She
waited anxiously for his reaction.

He said nothing. Except for his quickened breath, he
lay silent and curiously still. Stefanie bit her lip and
fought down a feeling of panic. What if he couldn't
accept it—it could be too much too soon.

Jesse, she begged silently. Oh, Jesse—please don't let
me down now! Unable to bear his lack of response any
longer and dreading what it must mean, she rolled away
from him. 'I'm sorry, Jesse,' she said, her voice muffled
by the pillow. 'I—I can understand if you don't want
it.' It was hard to say the words.

'Don't want it!' He came to life and grabbed her by
the shoulders and turned her roughly to him. 'Don't say
that, Stefanie. Don't ever say that!'

She stared at him, eyes wide and more than a little
frightened by the strength of his reaction to the words
she had spoken with reluctance.

Jesse groaned and pulled her back into his arms. 'I'm
sorry, sweetheart,' he murmured, kissing her brow in
apology. 'You can't possibly know . . .' His voice trailed
off.

'Know what, Jesse?'

He moved restlessly on the crumpled sheet. 'Wanda
was pregnant once,' he said without expression. 'I'd had
about two months to get used to the idea. Even found
myself looking at teddy bears and hockey sticks,' he
added dryly.

'What happened?' Stefanie watched his face in the
dim light from the street. 'Did she have a mis-
carriage?'

'Abortion.' The word hung stark and hard in the dark. 'She didn't want it, and didn't care that I did.' Stefanie could see the old pain etched on his face.

'Our marriage was pretty shaky at that point, and I guess she felt she had cause. But I asked her—begged her—not to do it. I told her that if we couldn't work things out I would raise the child myself. I thought I'd convinced her.' Jesse stopped for a moment and stared into the dark corners of the room, remembering the helpless horror of that time. 'She went away one weekend,' he finally continued in flat tones, 'and got rid of it.'

'Jesse,' said Stefanie softly, sitting up on the bed, 'come with me.' She took his hand and tugged impatiently.

Jesse frowned in puzzlement. 'Where?'

'Not far.'

He got up slowly and grasped her shoulders in a tight grip. 'Stefanie—about the baby . . .'

She raised her hand to his lips and silenced him. 'Hush, Jesse,' she said softly, and took him by the hand. She opened the door to the baby's room and turned on the dimmer switch just enough for a soft glow to light the room. She wanted him to see just how much she wanted his child, and no one seeing this room would ever doubt it.

The walls were painted a soft white, one of them with a springtime mural of frolicking lambs and rainbow skies. A huge Winnie-the-Pooh bear sat in one corner with stuffed arms out stretched and welcoming. A waiting cradle rested in the middle of the floor with a tiny patchwork quilt tucked in firmly. Stained glass butterflies swayed gently over the window, waiting to catch the morning sun. It was a soft and charming room that spoke of her love for their unborn child.

She turned to Jesse and reached up to stroke his silent face. 'I love you so much, Jesse,' she said softly. 'How could I not love your child?'

He exhaled a long and shaky breath. Kneeling down in front of her, he pressed his lips to her nurturing womb. As he stood up, he wrapped his arms tightly around her and buried his face in the soft darkness of her hair, whispering fervid words of love against her soft skin.

'Marry me soon, love,' he murmured. 'Very soon.'

'Yes, Jesse,' she said.

HARLEQUIN
PREMIERE AUTHOR EDITIONS

6 EXCITING HARLEQUIN AUTHORS —6 OF THEIR BEST BOOKS!

Daphne Clair
A STREAK OF GOLD

Marjorie Lewty
TO CATCH A BUTTERFLY

Anne Mather
SCORPIONS' DANCE

Jessica Steele
SPRING GIRL

Margaret Way
THE WILD SWAN

Violet Winspear
DESIRE HAS NO MERCY

Harlequin is pleased to offer these six very special titles, out of print since 1980. These authors have published over 250 titles between them. Popular demand required that we reissue each of these exciting romances in new beautifully designed covers.

Available in April wherever paperback books are sold, or through Harlequin Reader Service. Simply send your name, address and zip or postal code, with a check or money order for $2.50 for each copy ordered (includes 75¢ for postage and handling) payable to Harlequin Reader Service, to:

Harlequin Reader Service

In the U.S.
P.O. Box 52040
Phoenix, AZ 85072-2040

In Canada
P.O. Box 2800
Postal Station A
5170 Yonge Street
Willowdale, Ontario
M2N 6J3

PAE-1

EYE OF THE STORM

MAURA SEGER

A powerful
portrayal of
the events of
World War II in the
Pacific, *Eye of the Storm* is a riveting story of how love
triumphs over hatred. Aboard a ship steaming toward
Corregidor, Army Lt. Maggie Lawrence meets Marine Sgt.
Anthony Gargano. Despite military regulations against frater-
nization, they resolve to face together whatever lies ahead....
A searing novel by the author named by *Romantic Times* as
1984's Most Versatile Romance Author.

4 FREE
Harlequin Romances